D1546370

Married in Montana

MARRIED
IN
MONTANA

A Paradise Valley Ranch Romance

JANE PORTER

TULE
PUBLISHING

Dedication

Thank you to all the amazing book girls
who encourage and inspire
and love talking story.
And with special thanks to my brave first readers
Lee, Elisabeth, and Michelle
For being honest even when it hurts
Grateful thanks to Shevawn
For keeping the home fires burning
And finally thanks and kudos to Meghan
Tule's Managing Editor
For also brilliantly managing me

March 1890

Chapter One

Marietta, Montana – March 19, 1890

IT WAS ALL very well to be popular and in demand, but this was almost ridiculous. The tiny shop for Johanna Design on Main Street was standing room only today as apparently every woman in Marietta had come to Johanna's for a fitting this afternoon, filling every chair, stool, and sofa cushion.

Pressing two fingers to her throbbing temple, Ellie Burnett wished she could make a hasty exit, but she'd come to town expressly for the purpose of having the final fitting of her Easter dress, and as it was a ninety-minute drive each way from her father's ranch in Paradise Valley in good weather, she couldn't just leave and return later. The road through the valley could be treacherous, particularly in sleet, snow, or rain, with mountain run off flooding the Yellowstone River and, yes, the sun was shining right now, but Montana weather was mercurial, and the gusting winds could blow storm clouds through at any moment. And then there was her ill father and how difficult it was to leave him... how guilty she felt each time she left him...

She drew a slow breath, trying to calm herself. Everything would be fine. Everything would work out. She'd get her Easter dress, and she'd look fresh and desirable. *Marriageable.* Because God knew she needed a husband, and fast.

Her stomach churned at the thought and, suddenly overly warm, she unbuttoned the lapel of her coat, and drew another breath, willing herself to calm down. Hysterics were never appealing, much less in a room crowded with women. What she needed to do was focus on her goal of securing the right proposal. It shouldn't be this hard. Montana was full of single men. All she needed was one good man... that didn't make her skin crawl.

Ellie was reaching for another coat button when a very harried Johanna Douglas appeared from behind a brocade curtain, cheeks flushed, wisps of dark honey hair falling free from her chignon.

Ladies surged toward Johanna and the modiste dealt with each politely but firmly, even as she walked quickly toward Ellie. "It's not ready," Johanna said softly, taking Ellie's arm, drawing her away from the others. "I'm so sorry. If I could have sent word, I would have."

"Nothing is ready?"

"The jacket could be. In an hour, or two, probably two. But that is all I have for you to try on. Everything else is still in pins." Johanna squeezed her arm. "I am so, so sorry. I know this isn't a good time for you, either—"

"It's fine." Ellie exhaled and forced a smile, hiding her

disappointment. She couldn't, wouldn't, make Johanna, not only the best seamstress in Marietta, but Ellie's closest friend, feel bad. "I think that also means there's no time for tea."

"Oh, and how I'd love to sit for a bit and catch up. You have no idea how much I'd love a good gossip right now. The things I could tell you!" Johanna wrapped her arm around Ellie and gave her a quick squeeze. "I do miss you."

"It's a shame you're just so good at what you do."

Johanna laughed, just as Ellie intended. "Come back Friday, if you can," Johanna said, even as she lifted a hand to stop a customer from interrupting. "I promise to have it done then."

"I'll see what I can do."

"And if that doesn't work, I'll come to you. Sinclair and McKenna have been pestering Mama and me to come for supper so it wouldn't be a problem."

"You're already so busy—"

"Never too busy for you." She linked arms with Ellie and they squeezed through the crowd, heading for the door. Johanna's voice dropped to a whisper as she asked, "Ellie, how is your father? I'm worried."

Ellie's throat tightened. "I'm worried, too."

"Oh dear."

"We knew this was inevitable, but I see the writing on the wall now, and it's terrifying." Eyes burning, Ellie blinked hard. The relentless weight in her chest made breathing difficult, never mind talking. She couldn't imagine the future without her larger than life father. It had just been the two of them since she was five and her mother died in childbirth, the baby buried with her in the cemetery. "No one still knows, though, but you, and I'm so grateful you've kept our secret."

"Why unleash the wolves?" Johanna said sympathetically. "If men understood your situation they'd take advantage of it and that's not the kind of husband you want to attract. Fortunately, you are strong. Stronger than any woman I know," she added, giving Ellie a swift, fierce hug.

Ellie held back the sting of tears and managed a mocking smile. "I have to be. Papa wouldn't have it any other way."

"There's the Ellie Burnett backbone I know and love." Johanna opened the door. "But I am sorry to have wasted your time today. I really thought your dress would be ready but customers keep dropping in. Easter has become so busy, and even though I've been working nonstop, it's not enough, not even with Mother's help."

Ellie began tugging on her gloves. "You'd said her eyes are becoming a problem."

"She can cut the fabric and do hems and seams, but I can't rely on her for the finer needlework. But next year it will be different, I promise. Now that I know the Easter dress is a thing here, too, and not just in New York."

Ellie snorted. "I can't believe Marietta has its own Easter parade."

"You don't intend to parade down Main Street and over

to the Graff in your new gown?"

"Of course not! That would be foolish. I'll be seen at the Graff, enjoying the Easter dinner buffet with you, not traipsing down dirty Main Street in my finest."

Johanna bit into her lip. "Ellie, Sin has already invited Mama and me to be his guests for dinner, but I'm sure Sinclair would be happy to have you join his table, too. Should I ask him?"

"No," Ellie said crossly, stepping outside onto the sidewalk. "It would be awkward for all, don't you think?"

Johanna remained on the threshold. "Not necessarily. He's happily married—"

"Yes, and he was my fiancé before he married her!" Ellie flushed, her cheeks annoyingly hot. She hated still being so sensitive about the broken engagement. "I know he was mine for all of five minutes but, *still*, it stings."

"You'll find the right man."

"Hmph! My options are looking grim. But then you know I love a good challenge." And then she gave Johanna a quick kiss on the cheek and a jaunty wave, and was off to untie Oisin from the hitching post.

Ellie lifted her elegant skirts with one hand and climbed into her smart black buggy. She shot a glance up, taking in the clouds sailing overhead, and then set off, leaving Marietta at a brisk speed, eager to escape town and the uncomfortable memories stirred up by her conversation with Johanna.

Last fall, Johanna's brother, Sinclair, had been the perfect suitor, and he would have been the perfect husband, too, but, by abruptly marrying his childhood sweetheart, the Copper King Patrick Frasier's daughter McKenna, at Christmas instead of Ellie, Sinclair had embarrassed her, leaving her in the lurch.

It had been three months since then and Ellie still needed a husband, and there was nothing she hated more than being on the marriage mart, particularly when one didn't just want a husband, but needed one, urgently. Those were not good conditions for a satisfying courtship.

Spotting a slow moving wagon in front of her, Ellie cracked her whip above her stallion's ears, spurring Oisin faster so they could pass, and they did, most impressively, despite the strong wind whistling through the valley from Yellowstone. The wind was as much a part of Paradise Valley as the mountains and the river and strangers always remarked on the gusts, but she loved them. They made her feel unfettered and free—

From beneath the carriage came a low, shuddering crack and then the carriage lurched. Ellie threw out her hands to brace herself as the buggy suddenly tipped over but there was no way to stop from being flung out. For a moment she was flying through the air and then in the next, she slammed into the ground. The impact knocked the wind from her and she lay stunned and shaken, struggling to catch her breath.

What had just happened?

Blinking she looked toward her gleaming carriage, now

sideways in the dirt. Oisin remained in place, appearing as confused as she felt.

Drawing another slow breath, Ellie wiggled her toes and then gingerly moved her arms and legs. Nothing seemed to be broken. Thank God. Who would take care of Papa if she ended up in a plaster?

Still trying to gather herself, she heard the jingle of a horse and the creak of a wagon slowing near her buggy. Pride kicked in. The last thing she wanted was to be found in a heap, in a ditch. She struggled to rise but her ankle buckled and she fell back onto her rear end, wincing.

"That was stupid," a deep rough male voice said curtly. "You're lucky you're not dead."

She couldn't see his face, not with the sun in her eyes and the brim of his hat shading his features, but she heard the accent. A lilting Irish brogue. He hadn't been born in Montana, or anywhere else in America. It didn't help that the stranger dwarfed her—his shoulders were immense—forcing her to tip her head back to look into his face.

"Thank you for your courtesy. No need to assist me to my feet," she retorted, biting down to muffle the groan of pain as she staggered up once more, this time determined to stick. The world swam a bit, nausea rushing through her as she tried to put weight on her right foot. But she wasn't going to let him know how much her ankle pained her.

He practically growled as he took her elbow, steadying her. "You're hurt." From someone else the tone would be one of concern. From him, it was an accusation.

She could feel the heat and pressure of his hand even through her coat and she didn't like it. "I'm fine." She tried to shake him off. "Let me see to my horse."

"He's in better shape than you," he answered flatly, releasing his hold.

"How do you know?"

"I checked on him first."

"A true gallant," she muttered, brushing off her dirty skirt and then her scraped hands. She was lucky it hadn't snowed or rained in the past week, otherwise she'd be covered in mud.

"He shouldn't be punished for your recklessness," he said, moving toward her buggy.

She glared at the Irishman's departing back. His leather coat clung to the broad planes of his shoulders and torso, while his black hair hung in long waves to his shoulders. "I'm not reckless."

"Then you lack skill, because you can't drive. You're a danger to all."

Outraged, she limped toward her horse. "You don't know the first thing about me," she said, moving around her stallion, stroking Oisin's flank and then his belly, and finally his shoulder. Thankfully, Oisin had come through unscathed.

The Irishman watched her as she completed her inspection. "I know enough to have kept my distance," he said as she gave the stallion a last pat on the shoulder.

Ellie shot him a sharp glance. "What does that mean?"

"I understood you were quite intelligent. I'm sure you don't need me to spell it out," he said, taking off his hat to drag a hand through thick black hair, pushing the locks back from his brow.

Without the hat he looked different.

Without the hat he looked… familiar.

An uneasy sensation ricocheted through her as their gazes met and held. Oh no. No. It was *him*. The fireman from the night of her doomed engagement party last December.

She gulped a breath, cheeks hot, a frisson of awareness racing through her. She'd only seen him that one night, briefly, and then not since. She'd wondered where he'd gone and why he hadn't attended any of the events in Marietta and, yet, here he was, on the side of the road, on the way to Emigrant.

She swallowed hard as she scanned his face. No wonder he'd made such an impression. Even in the afternoon sunlight, his eyes were dark, nearly as black as his hair, and his face was all hard, masculine edges and angles—high cheekbones, strong jaw, straight nose, firm lips.

Just looking at him made her chest grow tight. Her heart did a funny little beat. "We've never met," she murmured, because that was also true. She'd seen him on the fire wagon when all hell was breaking loose, but they hadn't spoken.

"Never have been introduced, no, but you're Archibald

Burnett's daughter."

It was impossible to ignore the coolness in his voice. "Do you not like my father?"

"I don't know a single man in this valley who doesn't respect him."

So this was about her. Interesting. She lifted her chin a fraction, expression challenging. "You've formed an opinion about me, then."

"I have."

"Unflattering it seems."

"There's no point to this. You're already defensive."

Her face prickled with heat. She ground her teeth together, forcing a smile, aware her strong personality rubbed some the wrong way, and yet she didn't try to be offensive, she just wanted to be herself. But people loved having opinions and they loved to judge.

"I'm not allowed to know why you're so critical?" she asked. "Unless this is about how I handle a horse? Perhaps you're one of those old-fashioned men who don't approve of women driving fast."

"Indeed. I prefer a woman to be a lady."

Ah. So he was one of those that liked to judge. Good to know. "And how am I not a lady?"

"You're too obvious."

"I beg your pardon?"

"You're husband hunting, Miss Burnett."

Her face burned but she wouldn't let him know she was

embarrassed. "Most young women hope to marry."

His big shoulders shifted. "With you being more... *determined*... than most."

She lifted a quelling brow but he merely shrugged.

"You'd be more successful, Miss Burnett, if you started behaving more like a lady."

"I do not know what you mean."

"No? Stop acting as if you wear the trousers."

Ellie went hot and then cold. For a moment she couldn't think of a single thing to say, and then her shock gave way to rage. She drew a quick breath, fingers curling into a fist. If he were shorter, she'd slap him, as it was, she'd never reach his face. "What I do, and how I do it, is none of your concern, Mister...."

"Sheenan."

"So, please continue on, Mr. Sheenan, as neither your assistance or opinions are required. Good day."

He didn't go. He stood off to the side watching her.

She was determined to ignore him and so she focused on Oisin, her beloved black stallion given to her for her twenty-first birthday last summer. Oisin wasn't just her favorite horse, he was one of her best friends and while he was unscathed, her carriage wasn't so lucky, the axle had snapped in two.

The broken axle meant the carriage couldn't be moved, but she could unharness Oisin and ride him bareback home. It wouldn't be the first time, and no matter what this

Sheenan thought of her, she was an excellent horsewoman. Her father, Archibald Burnett of Fort Worth, Texas, one of the original cowboys on the Bozeman cattle drive, wouldn't have it any other way. A single father, he'd made sure she could ride and rope as well as any man, determined his daughter would survive life in Montana's rugged Paradise Valley.

Aware that Mr. Sheenan was waiting for her to fall apart, she set to work unbuckling the leather harness. She crooned to Oisin as she worked, and gradually her hands stopped trembling, her nerves replaced by indignation as she peeled away the belly band and breastplate, leaving just the driving bit in place.

Mr. Sheenan was not a gentleman. He should have aided her, not simply stood back and watched. Sinclair would have helped her—

She broke off, jaw grinding tight, the ache in her ankle increasing by the second.

She couldn't focus on the pain, though, and she didn't want to think about Sinclair Douglas, either, or the fact that she had to have had the shortest engagement in Marietta's history.

Taking the driving bridle lines in hand, she drew Oisin parallel to the buggy and used the buggy's high step to seat herself. Oisin didn't even twitch a muscle or flick his tail as she adjusted her swollen ankle and then settled her gown's full skirts, giving them an elegant shake.

It was then, and only then, that she looked over at Mr. Sheenan. The late afternoon sun's bright rays gilded him with light, preventing her from seeing his expression, but she certainly hoped he could see hers because she felt beyond insulted. She was livid. "As I said, there was no need to trouble yourself, Mr. Sheenan. And, for your information, trousers do not make a man. Next time you meet a lady in distress, try some chivalry. Goodbye."

And then with a flick of the lines, Oisin was off, delighted to be free of the buggy. She let him run, too, even though the canter bounced her ankle, but she was anxious to put distance between her and the arrogant Irishman and she'd suffer a little pain if it meant she could leave him in the dust.

The wind tugged at her hat, loosening the ribbons to the point that she shoved it back, letting it fall behind her head. Her long hair pulled free of the pins and by the time she reached the wood and iron gate marking the entrance to the Burnett Ranch she knew she looked completely disheveled but she also felt completely, gloriously free.

Once inside the impressive gate, she slowed to a walk, letting Oisin cool down. "Well done, my love," she said, smiling and patting his warm damp neck. "We made record time today, even without a saddle."

As the sturdy two-story split-log house with the square dormer windows came into view, Ellie did her best to tidy her hair, braiding the thick red mass before coiling it and pinning it beneath her bonnet. She'd enjoyed her wild ride, but her father wouldn't be pleased if she returned from Marietta looking like a banshee. She knew of banshees of course because her mother's family, the Henleys, had been Irish, having sailed from Galway seventy-five years ago to settle in Boston.

Her father's family were English, but he'd raised Ellie on the Gaelic fairy tales and myths her mother used to tell her, which was why Ellie had named her stallion Oisin. Oisin being the son of the great warrior Fionn MacCool and the goddess Sive.

Ellie embraced all things Irish, with the exception of Mr. Sheenan. He was the one Irishman she disliked intensely.

Home, she was greeted by a stable hand who promptly took the reins from her, and then helped her down. She shared what had happened to the buggy, expressing her surprise and concern that a new buggy should suffer axle failure so soon after its purchase, especially as it was supposed to be brand new. The stable hand promised to take it up with Mr. Harrison, the ranch manager, and she gave directions on where the broken buggy could be found.

Ellie then struggled not to limp her way into the house, anxious to check on her father. She discovered him in the parlor in his favorite chair, his legs up on an ottoman, a blanket over his lap. She didn't know how it was possible, but he looked even frailer than he had this morning when she'd set off for Marietta.

It was on the tip of her tongue to tell him about her adventures—or misadventures, including her concern that an expensive new buggy had such a serious defect—when something in his expression made her hold the words back.

She moved to his side, taking small steps to hide her throbbing ankle. "Are you hurting terribly, Papa?" she asked, gently laying a hand to his brow and then his cheek.

"No more than usual," he said gruffly, but the tiny white lines at his mouth and the deeper creases at his eyes gave him away.

"I don't believe you," she answered, lightly smoothing his bushy white and silver goatee, the perfect partner for his white handlebar moustache. He had a grand moustache. He'd always been quite proud of it, keeping the points meticulously shaped and waxed. "Should I send for the doctor?"

"Why? What will he do? There's nothing anyone can do."

"We can still go to New York. There's that Dr. Coley in Manhattan—"

"There is nothing for him to amputate. Not unless you're ready to be rid of me."

The very idea made her chest ache. "Never!" She reached out to cover his hands with hers, his skin cool and thin beneath hers. "But he's doing some experimental treatments—"

"I wouldn't survive the trip east, Ellie. Turns out I can barely manage a walk around the barn."

Understanding dawned. "Is that what you did today? Is that why you're so tired?"

"I needed to let Harrison know to drive some of the sheep from the upper pasture."

"You couldn't send Mrs. Baxter?"

"She left early. One of the girls took sick."

"Papa, what was so important that you couldn't wait for me to come home?"

"I've got a young fellow who works for Avon Gilmore coming to pick up a dozen sheep. I wanted our Harrison to move them from the back pasture toward the house to make it easier."

"This young fellow is coming today?"

"Should be here anytime now."

Ellie suddenly had a sneaking suspicion she knew who the farmer might be, and she shuddered as she pictured massive shoulders, black hair, and a pair of unsmiling dark eyes. "Tell me he's not Irish."

"Thomas Sheenan is Irish." Archibald's eyes narrowed. "Why? What's wrong with him?"

She wasn't even sure how to explain what had happened on the road from Marietta. "I passed him earlier."

"And?"

"I don't like him."

"Why not? What did he do? Run you off the road?"

Her face warmed. "No. *I* had an accident. The buggy's axle broke, and I don't understand how as it's supposed to be new, but when it cracked the wheel came off and I went sailing into a rut next to the road." She drew a short, livid breath. "He witnessed the entire thing, and he stopped, but he wasn't interested in helping. He was quite rude, actually."

Her father frowned. "What did he do?"

"*Nothing.* That's just my point. He stopped, but once he saw I hadn't killed myself, instead of assisting me to my feet, he lectured me on my poor driving skills." She felt her pulse quicken. She told herself it was because he'd been critical and overbearing and nothing to do with the fact that he was the handsome fireman she'd seen last December. She'd had dreams about the fireman, but her dreams were far nicer than the reality. "He knew I was your daughter, too, which makes it all the more aggravating."

"I don't know why you care what he thinks." Archibald tipped his head back and closed his eyes, and drew a slow shallow breath. The air rattled in his lungs, making a faint wheezy sound. "You don't have to socialize with him."

"I know, but who leaves a lady lying in the dirt—"

"Did he not offer to help in any way?"

"Oh, he halfheartedly took my elbow at one point, but it was only after I'd given him a setdown."

"I'm sure it was quite a setdown, too."

"But it made no impression on him, Papa. He's altogether too rude and too arrogant."

"I hope his high-handed manners will not offend the sheep."

She straightened, arms crossing over her chest. "I'm serious."

"So am I. You're not a sheep. You don't have to like him." He opened his eyes, his gaze meeting hers. "Unless you'd hoped to make a suitor out of him?"

Heat washed through her and she felt her cheeks flame. "Heavens, no! As you said, I'm not a sheep."

"Speaking of livestock, I've had two recent offers for the ranch. One is quite fair—"

"No, Papa. We already discussed this. We're not selling, and I wish you hadn't put the word out that you were considering returning to Texas. It doesn't aid my case."

"It's better than letting them know I'm dying."

"Yes, but we want a suitor that would like to work the ranch with me, not someone to replace us here."

"But if you can't find a suitor soon, you won't be living here, not after I'm gone."

"I had a suitor."

"Douglas didn't work out and that ended months ago. Perhaps you need to stop being so particular and accept one."

Her lips compressed as she bit back her frustration. Her father had been quite progressive until recently. "Old age is making you old-fashioned," she said, limping to the hearth to add a log to the fire, before taking an iron to poke at the embers, creating a shower of sparks. "I don't know why you think I couldn't manage here alone."

"Are you hurt?"

"No."

"You're walking oddly."

"It's nothing. It'll go away."

"Did that happen in the fall?"

"It wasn't a fall. I was thrown." She gave the embers another fierce jab, her frustration getting the better of her. "Quite spectacularly."

"Then it's a good thing you weren't seriously injured. Have you sent someone to retrieve the buggy?"

"I have. But they may not be able to do anything until tomorrow."

"I'd like to see the axle. It's supposed to be new."

"I thought the same thing. And, Papa, I can manage here. You know I can—"

"Not alone. Not after I'm gone. You don't know men."

She shot him a sharp glance. "I know you, and if I could manage you—"

"This is different. I'm your father, not a… not a—"

"What?"

"Randy stallion."

"Papa!"

"But it's true. You're too young, and far too pretty. Your mama was far too pretty, too, and it's a danger. Living here, alone, you'd be a target for every unscrupulous man, and I have not spent my life protecting you, only to leave you vulnerable now."

"Then don't die. It's most inconvenient."

He smiled crookedly and watched as she returned the poker iron to the fire tools. "You look just like her. Same glorious hair. Same sea green eyes."

"But I'm not as sweet, I know." She crossed to his side, kissed the top of his head. "You must feel absolutely miserable if you're being sentimental. Why won't you take some laudanum?"

"Won't touch the stuff. Need to keep my wits about me."

"For what, Papa? An Irishman who is coming to collect some sheep?"

"Pretty soon I won't feel pain. At least this way I know I'm still alive."

Ellie struggled to breathe around the lump filling her throat. "You're making me sad."

"That's why we need to get you settled. We're running out of time."

She couldn't answer, not when fear filled her throat and made her chest ache. He was so much weaker today than yesterday, and yesterday he'd been exhausted and frail. She couldn't imagine a week from now. And a month?

She blinked hard, trying to clear the sting from her eyes. "Can I get you something? Have you had—" She broke off, listening to the voices outside.

They both listened. Ellie's stomach rose and fell. "I think he's here," she said.

Archibald struggled to fold his blanket. "Well, go on up."

"Up?" she repeated, taking the blanket from him and swiftly folding it into neat squares.

"Yes, up. Upstairs. That way you won't have to deal with him again."

"And how do you intend to manage? You can't even get out of your chair, Papa."

"Someone will send him through eventually."

He was a dreadful, stubborn old man and she loved him more than life itself. "I'll act as your hostess."

"But don't you want to go hide?"

"And when have I ever hid from anyone, or anything?" She gave him a reproving look. "Because I haven't, and I'm not about to start now."

A hard knock sounded on the front door. Ellie smoothed the front of her skirt. "I shall let the pig farmer in."

"He's not a pig farmer."

"Apologies, mutton." She swept away with as much dignity as she could muster, considering her tender ankle, and headed for the front door.

CHAPTER TWO

THE DOOR OPENED and she was there, in her green dress with the mud splatters, her thick red hair half braided, the rest spilling over her shoulders and down her back. She looked up at him, delicate winged brows arching in disdain. She wasn't surprised to see him, which meant her father had prepared her.

"Mr. Sheenan," she said coolly.

"Miss Burnett," he replied, inclining his head.

He noticed she didn't invite him in. He suspected if she had her way she'd leave him on the doorstep forever.

"You arrived home in one piece," he said.

Her chin went up, eyes flashing fire. "Did you think I wouldn't?"

"I was prepared for the worst."

"How disappointing for you then."

If he were a man that smiled, he might have smiled then. "Your man said your father is inside. Does he wish to speak to me, or is he good with me collecting the livestock and returning home?"

"He's in the parlor," she said, not bothering to open the

door wider, or step back to allow him to pass.

She was being deliberately difficult, wasting his time, trying to make him feel small. Perhaps he should be offended. Perhaps he should feel insulted and small.

He didn't.

While it was true the days were still short, and night came quickly, Ellie Burnett heated his blood, making him hard and carnal. "I don't know where the parlor is."

She gave him a look he couldn't decipher. "You do not have parlors in Ireland?"

"*We* did not," he answered, his gaze traveling slowly, lazily over her flawless face, as if she was his to study and explore.

He knew she didn't like it, and yet it was a pleasure looking at her. Ivory skin, green eyes, lush, dark pink mouth. He'd like that mouth on him. If she weren't Archibald Burnett's virgin daughter he'd have her on her knees. Or on her back, skirts up, thighs parted.

He grew hotter, harder, making him wish he could adjust himself since his trousers had become unbearably tight in all the wrong places.

Maybe it was time to visit the brothel above Grey's Saloon or, better yet, find a widow who'd enjoy physical pursuits without ties. Thomas didn't want a relationship, and he certainly wasn't interested in virgins, marriage, or children. But he did enjoy bedding a beautiful, spirited woman, and Ellie with her thick, gleaming hair and oval face, was both beautiful and fierce.

"Then, please, let me help you," she said coolly, mockingly. "I'd hate for you to feel overwhelmed by a big house."

She turned around, skirts swishing. He followed her, liking the back view nearly as much as the front. If he was a gentleman, he wouldn't look.

He wasn't a gentleman.

Thank God.

"My father is under the weather today," she said, hesitating outside a closed door. "I ask that you be mindful of his health."

When he didn't answer, she added, "He's not contagious, if that's what you're thinking. I'm simply trying to be sure that he isn't overtired."

She didn't know that he knew. Her father had confided in him a week ago when Thomas made the final payment for the livestock. Burnett hadn't asked Thomas to keep the information private, but he had. It wasn't his secret to share, and the news would influence the suitors lining up for Miss Burnett's hand. He didn't want to marry her but, at the same time, there was no point making it harder for her to find a decent match. "I won't be long."

She gave him a speculative glance before her gleaming red head inclined. "Thank you." And then with her chin up and shoulders squared, she opened the door for him. "Mr. Sheenan is here, Papa."

Thomas moved past her, crossing the room to shake

Archibald's hand. "Good afternoon, sir."

"Coffee, or tea, Thomas?" the old man asked, voice raspy.

"Only if you want something. I don't intend to stay more than a few minutes."

Burnett turned to his daughter. "Tea, Ellie, please. And scones or biscuits if Mrs. Baxter made any fresh today."

Ellie shot Thomas a sharp look before walking out, leaving the door open.

Archibald gestured with a trembling hand to the door. "Close it. She doesn't need to know everything I say or do."

Thomas obliged, shutting the door gently. He returned to the hearth. "She's protective of you."

"I've given her a great deal of freedom." Archibald's forehead creased, his thick salt and pepper hair falling forward. He combed it back irritably. "I don't mind dying. But I do mind leaving her to the wolves."

"She'll find it hard in the beginning, but she's stronger than you think."

Archibald stared at him hard. "What happened on the road today?"

"She told you."

"She tells me everything."

"Then she told you she rode like the devil was chasing her."

"Ellie enjoys the wind in her hair."

Thomas grimaced. "That's one way of putting it."

"How would you put it?"

"She's willful. Spoiled."

"That she is. But she's also smart, smarter than most men around here, and it's going to cause problems for her."

"Why are you telling me this?"

"You know why."

"I'm not the marrying kind."

"Why not? Do you fancy men?"

"I don't fancy men. I like bedding women. I'd bed your daughter. But I'd never offer for her." He met the Texan's narrowed gaze and held it. "Not trying to be disrespectful, just clear about my position. I came to Montana to get away from family. The last thing I want to do is start one."

"What was wrong with your family? Abusive pa? Unfeeling ma?"

Thomas pictured his village and the small stone house that had been home. And then he pictured the undertaker coming again, and again, and again. How many people could you bury before you had enough of the living? "That's personal."

The Texan ran an unsteady hand over his moustache. "I need to ask you a favor."

"As long as you're not asking me to marry your daughter."

"She'd be a good wife."

"If you like hellcats."

Archibald laughed hoarsely, and then the laugh turned to

a cough and he coughed until tears streamed from his eyes. The door opened and Ellie was there, running to her father's side, trying to adjust his position while shooting Thomas a furious look.

She blamed him, which was fine. He didn't need or want her to like him. It was better if she didn't, and safer if she kept her distance.

She wasn't safe with him. He'd wanted her from the first moment he saw her, back in early November, the day Montana became a state. He'd been on the fire wagon with the other volunteer firemen as it paraded down Main Street during the statehood celebrations. She was on the street, near the Bank of Marietta, watching the parade with a friend. The friend was blonde and curvy and pretty, but he'd only had eyes for the tall, slender redhead.

He'd watched her intently, liking everything about her, from the tilt of her lips, to the angle of her jaw, to the way she'd watched the parade as though she could do better, and had seen better. From the expensive cut of her coat and hat, he was certain she had seen better. He was certain, too, from the haughty lift of her chin, and the slightly bored expression in her light eyes, that she believed she deserved better, at least better than Marietta, not that Marietta was anything to sneer at, not compared to the places he'd been and things he'd seen.

He didn't know her story, but it wasn't hard to imagine. She came from money, and she carried herself like a princess, and she was waiting for her prince, only he hadn't shown up yet.

Her prince would be tall and fair and have exquisite manners. He'd place her on a pedestal and treat her like a lady, and would eventually bore her to tears but, by then, she'd be Mrs. Charming and fat with his brats and the haughty tilt of her chin would turn to grim resignation and anger because she wanted more out of life and she'd gotten less.

Women like her didn't understand that if they wanted less, they'd end up with more. Maybe one only understood such a thing if they'd grown up hungry and poor.

Ellie glared at him now over her father's head. "I think you should go," she said, a hand on her father's back.

Still coughing, Archibald shook his head. "We haven't had our tea."

"He can have tea at home, Papa."

"No. He is having tea with me." Archibald struggled to get the words out. "So bring the tea and biscuits, Ellie. Stop the chatter and dillydallying."

"I'm not chattering or dillydallying, Papa."

"But you are arguing." He sputtered, between shallow breaths of air. "And arguing is a form of dallying."

"Of course, Papa. What am I thinking?" She shot Thomas another livid look before marching out, slamming the door behind her.

Archibald winced at the slam and then tugged on his

goatee. "She takes after her mother."

"In looks or temperament?"

"Looks." The Texan's forehead furrowed. "She has my temperament."

"Is that why she is not yet betrothed?"

"She's had offers, including proposals from Denver and Butte, but she hasn't accepted any. She's particular."

"You mean, she likes to be in control."

"She's accustomed to having her way."

Thomas said nothing. There was no point. Ellie was not his concern. He was not getting involved.

"But you see my problem, don't you?" Archibald persisted.

"Yes, she's a problem."

For a moment the old Texan didn't seem to know how to respond, and then he smiled crookedly. "You would have been a good match for her—"

"No. Not so. I wouldn't put up with the attitude."

"She said you were rude to her today, on the road."

"She could have been killed. There was no need to push her horse. She could ease up with her whip."

"She loves that horse."

"Then she ought to slow down and put away the whip."

"She doesn't actually strike Oisin."

"No, she cracks it above his ears, which is absurd when you have a young stallion. He already enjoys running. No need to frighten him."

"You know your horses?"

"I've been around them my whole life."

"Hmmm." Archibald studied him for a long moment. "You're an interesting fellow."

"Not that interesting."

"But practical. Maybe that's why I like you. I'm practical, too. Which is why I can't leave her out here, not after I'm gone."

Thomas bit his tongue to keep from saying anything else.

"She's young and wealthy. Very wealthy."

"I intend to earn my money, not marry it."

"There's no reason you can't do both."

Thomas said nothing. There was no point in responding. He'd only be wasting his breath.

Archibald shifted, wincing as he adjusted his position. "I need a favor."

"If it's related to the ranch, yes. If it's with regards to Miss Burnett, no."

"I need to show her something, but I can't drive her there myself. I can't travel anymore, not even into town. I want you to take her for me."

"I am sure there is someone better to accompany her."

"No one I can trust."

"You shouldn't trust me."

"You don't want her—"

"Let's be clear, Mr. Burnett. I want her, but I'm not going to make a play for her."

"That alone makes you trustworthy."

"Interesting logic."

Archibald smiled grimly. "Marrying her, you'd become one of the wealthiest men in Crawford and Park counties. By refusing to marry her, I know you're not driven by the dollar."

"I keep repeating myself but, if I get rich, I want to make it on my own."

"A principled man."

"No sir. I just don't like being beholden."

"Even better. We'll make it a business deal. Show her the house I've built for her on Bramble, this coming Sunday after church, and I'll add a dozen head to your herd. Your choice, cattle or sheep."

"That's overly generous. I'm not comfortable with the arrangement."

"And I'm not comfortable period. I'm dying. I want her settled by Easter—"

"That's just two weeks away."

"Exactly. I'll be lucky to last that long."

ELLIE POURED THE tea for her father and Mr. Sheenan and then left the parlor, unable to remain when her stomach was filled with knots.

She'd heard what her father said to the Irishman. She'd heard him clearly. Papa wanted her settled by Easter, because he doubted he'd live much longer. Easter was April sixth. Just a little over two weeks away.

A little over two weeks before she lost the only person she'd ever loved. It was inconceivable. Impossible to wrap her head around such a reality. She couldn't imagine her life without him. She'd be absolutely alone.

In the kitchen, Ellie reached for her old coat on the hook near the back door. Thrusting her arms into the sleeves, she fastened the thick buttons and went outside to get air. It was nearing dusk and just the top of Emigrant Peak glowed gold, catching the last of the day's rays of light, while the rest of the mountain range, like the valley, was already swathed in lavender shadows.

Outside, she walked in painful circles, from the house to the stables, and then around the barn, and back. Her ankle throbbed and her teeth chattered as she walked, but it was hard to get warm when she was so icy on the inside, chilled by her father's words. Fate wasn't fair. Or kind.

She was making another unhappy loop when she spotted the Irishman approaching the barn. His wagon was ready, the sheep already loaded and bleating plaintively in the back.

She lifted her chin and dropped her arms as he neared. "I hope you haven't worn him out."

He didn't immediately answer, his gaze shifting to the wagon and the milling sheep. She could have sworn he was counting them. Did he really think her father would swindle him? How offensive! He knew nothing about the Burnetts then, or honor. "They are all there, and healthy, too," she said curtly, not bothering to hide her irritation.

Thomas looked at her, expression blank. "He's beginning to fail."

"Yes, I know."

"Is there nothing that can be done?"

"No. Well, maybe, if we had gone to New York, maybe Dr. Coley might have been able to do something, but Papa wouldn't consider it. He said the trip was too far, and he didn't feel like being a pincushion."

"Who is this Dr. Coley?"

"He specializes in bone and soft tissue cancer. He's very experimental, not everyone approves of his methods, but he might have given my father a chance... as well as given me more time with him."

Thomas looked doubtful. "Or not. These new doctors kill more patients than they save."

"But he's going to die anyway, and if one of these new treatments might have worked... then how could we not try?" She sighed. "If it were up to me, we would have been in New York a year ago."

"He's asked me to show you something in town on Sunday, after church."

"You don't attend church."

"I don't attend St. James."

And then she understood. Of course. He was Catholic.

She gave him a hard look. "I don't need anyone to show

me anything, here or in town, and, if I needed an escort, it wouldn't be you."

"This isn't my idea, nor is it something I'm eager to do."

"So why do it?"

"He's compensating me well. Why else?"

"Of course." At least he was honest.

Her gaze held his. His eyes were nearly black in the lavender twilight. Today was the first time since she'd seen him since December, the night of the Frasier mine explosion and fire when he'd registered in a flash of quick sharp impressions—tall, thick hair, snapping black eyes in a hard masculine face—but her impressions hadn't been wrong.

He was dark and intense, hard and fierce, and nothing like her fair, blue-eyed fiancé, Sinclair Douglas.

Sinclair had left her in the middle of their engagement party to rush to the Frasier mine, even though he no longer worked for the Frasiers. She'd been hurt and furious and horrified, and she'd followed Sinclair out of the hotel and had begged him not to go, but Sinclair turned away even as she pleaded with him, and that was when she'd locked glances with the firefighter.

He'd heard her begging Sinclair. The firefighter had heard, she could tell, and he pitied her.

There was no reason for him to pity her.

Her chin had gone up and she'd thrown him a look of disdain because what else was she going to do? Cave? Cry? Break?

Never.

It had been a terrible night, and a horrific next day, and once everyone knew the engagement was over, a difficult Christmas and New Year. It had been months since the engagement party, and every time Ellie thought people had stopped talking about humiliation, she overheard someone whispering, *"You know Ellie Burnett lost her fiancé to that scandalous Frasier heiress…"*

She hated the chatter and speculation, but Marietta was a small town, and she supposed there weren't a lot of things for people to discuss besides the weather—cold, cold, and more cold—so whenever someone did say something to her, or about her, she lifted her chin, and smiled, a cool, proud, brazen smile because, after all, there were worse things than gossip, and worse things in a failed engagement. Worse things than shame.

There was death and loss. Grief.

Ellie was five when her mother died and she didn't re-member her mother, but she remembered the grief. She remembered the longing, and the missing, and how the missing filled her, aching within her, a void that couldn't be answered.

A void that wouldn't be soothed.

The grief had been a constant growing up, and even though it had been years since she ached, it was still there, a quiet companion. A shadow. She found that she pushed herself just because she had to push to actually feel something. Emotions didn't come easily to her, and she wasn't sure if that was because she took after her Texan father, or if because grieving had hardened her, but it probably wasn't important. The only thing important now, was saving the Burnett Ranch.

"Do you know what my father wants you to show me?" she asked after a long minute had passed.

"I do."

She hesitated, choosing her words with care. "Does this have to do with property on Bramble?"

Thomas's dark head turned, his intense gaze narrowed on her face. "You know."

"I know he's determined to see me settled. But I'm not interested—"

"How can you say that if you haven't seen it?"

"I'd hate life in Marietta."

"You wouldn't be lonely."

"I wouldn't have freedom."

He sighed and shook his head, expression grim. "I'll pick you up Sunday in front of the church, after the eleven a.m. service."

"WHAT ABOUT THE Irishman?" her father asked the next evening, breaking the silence.

Ellie's brow lifted. She looked up from her needlework. "What about him?" she asked, determined not to be short tempered even though sewing was one of her least favorite things to do. She wouldn't sew for anyone, and had adamantly refused from mending and doing even decorative needlework, but his favorite nightshirt had lost the second button and she couldn't wait for Mrs. Baxter to fix it. Time was in short supply for everything these days.

"Why isn't he a candidate?" her father asked mildly.

"Stop making it sound like an election. I'm not running for office, nor is he. I just want someone healthy and strong enough to do the work, and smart enough to know who is the boss." She gave him a level look. "And I think we both know Mr. Sheenan would not allow that."

"Have you asked him?"

She snorted. "He's already accused me of 'wearing the trousers.' I certainly have no desire to provide him additional ammunition."

"You don't think he could be a good husband?"

"*No.*" She checked the button and it seemed secure so she tied a knot and bit off the thread. "How can you like him, Papa?"

"He's smart, strong, young, ambitious, and honest."

"You failed to mention haughty, big-headed, egotistical—"

"I've been called all of those things, nearly all my life."

"Hmph." She rose and gave the shirt a shake. "I'll put this back in your wardrobe. It's ready to wear. And then I think I'll go to bed."

Archibald's brow arched. "You're giving up? Just like that?"

"I'm not giving up. I just don't feel like arguing with you."

But in her room, she couldn't climb into bed but her ankle was still too sore for her to pace. She wrapped a heavy wool shawl around her shoulders and took a seat on the cedar chest in front of her window and stared out at the moonlit landscape. It was a cloudless night and the stars were bright overhead, painting the barn and pastures a ghostly white below.

She'd arrived here with her mother as a toddler, having left Texas without any memories of the place. This ranch was all she'd ever known. And she understood she couldn't stop her father's cancer, but there was no reason she had to lose her only home, too.

Her father was leaving her plenty of money. She'd have more than she could ever spend, and the kind of security that meant she could do whatever she wanted... travel, build a fine house on the ranch, buy a second house somewhere else. But she didn't want a second house and she'd never felt any interest in traveling, at least not very far. She enjoyed visiting Butte and traveling to Bozeman, but her favorite escape was camping in Yellowstone, when her father would pitch a tent in a sagebrush meadow on the historic Bannock Trail. The meadow was filled with quaking aspen and Douglas firs and a gurgling stream on its way to meet the Yellowstone River.

They'd encountered all kinds of wildlife there—deer, bison, wolves, bears—but she'd never been afraid because her father wasn't afraid, and she didn't know if that was because he was an expert marksman, or if because like her, he relished adventure.

Ellie tipped her head against the glass, and squeezed her eyes closed. *Dear God, please take care of my father. Make sure he knows he was loved.*

CHAPTER THREE

THREE DAYS LATER, on Sunday morning, Ellie sat in the fifth row on the right side of St. James, the row she and her father always sat in, struggling to concentrate on the sermon when two of her current suitors sat in her line of sight. Mr. George Baker and Mr. Leeland Fridley.

Mr. Baker was a banker, not a baker. Short, bald, and a little soft around the middle, he was close to her age, maybe twenty-four, with the most unpleasant tendency to perspire heavily whenever near her. He didn't do it from a distance, just when speaking to her, and her father could blame Mr. Baker's nerves, but the last time Mr. Baker took her for a drive, she couldn't focus on anything but the beads of sweat rolling down his face. Damp palms were one thing, but a dripping brow was another.

Like Mr. Baker, Mr. Fridley had been raised somewhere on the East Coast. He'd arrived in Marietta with the first train and dealt in real estate. If you didn't know him personally, you might first think Leeland Fridley handsome, but on acquaintance he quickly became tiresome, overly preoccupied as he was with appearances, money, and public opinion.

So, which was the better suitor? The short, nervous, damp Mr. Baker, or the attractive but supercilious Leeland Fridley?

Mr. Fridley suddenly caught her eye and inclined his head. She stiffly nodded back, trying not to fixate on his dark hair, shiny with pomade. She couldn't imagine touching his hair. But then, was Mr. Baker's bald pate any better?

Easter was just two weeks away and she needed a third option. But where would this new suitor come from? She'd gone through seven or eight suitors since Christmas and each one seemed worse than the last. The problem wasn't entirely with the gentlemen, either. Ellie knew she wasn't a typical young woman, eager to marry and have a family. Her father had raised her as if she was a son, not a daughter. Growing up, he'd made sure she had good tutors, and he'd emphasized her need to read and write, as well as do advanced math so she could help him with his business. And she had helped. From the time she was sixteen, she'd taken care of his books, and placed his orders, and helped him make decisions regarding the future of the ranch. Three years ago when the horrific winter decimated Montana's cattle, cutting herds in half in parts of the state, the ranches in and around Yellowstone had been hit hard, where some ranchers lost ninety percent of their livestock.

They'd been far more fortunate at Burnett Ranch as they weren't as dependent on cattle as others. It had been Ellie who'd convinced her father several years earlier to diversify due to the continuing decline in the beef market. She'd run numbers to show him how sheep and hay crops could help them offset their losses, and so while the winter of 1886-1887 was bad, it wasn't nearly as devastating for them as it had been for their neighbors.

Ellie was proud of her business acumen, but when she tried to discuss business and ranching practices with her different suitors, it never went over well. Sinclair Douglas was perhaps the only one who had tolerated her opinions. The rest of the gentlemen were always eager to steer her back to proper topics like weather.

Or the next church picnic.

Ellie sighed inwardly, fingers lacing. If only she could be happy discussing weather and St. James's social events, but both topics were tedious. Being a lady was tiresome. She'd rather be on Oisin, riding hard, or traveling in her buggy with the wind pulling apart her hair, making her feel free.

She loved to be free.

Ellie blamed her father for that one.

But she wouldn't be free much longer. Certainly no husband would give her the freedom her father had allowed her.

Her heart did a funny flutter and she suddenly remembered Mr. Sheenan, and how he was to show her the property on Bramble.

Her stomach plummeted, intensifying the jitter in her veins.

Mr. Sheenan. He was not like any of her suitors. But

then, he was nothing like any of the men in Marietta.

She wasn't sure if that was a good thing, or not.

Her father had asked her several nights ago why the Irishman wasn't a candidate and she'd been appalled.

But, to be perfectly objective, why wasn't Mr. Sheenan? How could he be worse than Mr. Baker or Mr. Fridley? At least he had clean hair.

And broad shoulders. And an impressively fit physique. Not that she'd wanted to notice, but it was impossible to not be aware of his height and size when he'd loomed over her as she'd laid sprawled on the side of the road.

He should have helped her up.

She swallowed hard, hands gripping the prayer book in her lap. He was not a gentleman and she dreaded meeting him after this morning's service. Thomas Sheenan made her angry, as well as incredibly uneasy. Just looking at him made everything inside her lurch and slosh—most discomfiting.

He was also painfully arrogant but, in his defense, he wasn't vain or haughty like Mr. Fridley. Mr. Sheenan did no primping, prancing, or mincing. Nor did he sweat excessively.

His fault was the opposite. He was tall and muscular, darkly handsome, and absurdly confident. He exuded authority, oozing control, and it was beyond aggravating that a man who hadn't even been in Crawford County six months should have formed such a negative opinion of her.

How could he find fault with her behavior when he

didn't know her?

Pfft.

Ellie felt a prickle of awareness and she glanced from beneath her lashes to her left, and discovered that Mr. Baker was staring at her, full lips slightly parted, expression hungry.

She closed her eyes, and held her breath. *Please, dear Lord, send me a proper suitor. A man that I can respect and eventually tolerate in my bed. Amen.*

Prayer over, she opened her eyes and looked up at the pulpit from where the minister was *still* speaking. Normally she enjoyed attending the Sunday service, not because she was particularly religious, but it was a tradition in their family. Sunday was the one day her father didn't work as he made it a point of honoring the Sabbath. He did it for her late mother, part of the promise he'd made to her as she lay dying that he'd raised Ellie to be a good Christian. It was a big promise for Archibald to make since he wasn't a churchgoing man. But he'd kept his promise. Ellie never missed church, or the Sunday school classes after the worship service. He might feel like an imposter in the pew, but he made sure Ellie was there.

There was a ritual to attending church, too.

Growing up, after supper on Saturday night, he'd heat water for her bath, and then he'd wash her hair before sitting her before the hearth in her little rocking chair to ensure her long red hair dried completely before she went to bed. While her hair dried, he'd iron her best dress and her petticoats and then shine her shoes. Then on Sunday morning they'd put on their good clothes and head to town for church.

Papa gave Ellie her late mother's bible as a confirmation gift when she'd turned twelve. For nearly a year, Ellie poured over the bible, memorizing her mother's favorite underlined verses, but it had been a long time since Ellie believed that God answered prayers. If God did, he would have saved her father.

No one lived forever but, before the cancer, her father had been impossibly strong and healthy. At six-four he'd towered over men, and on the ranch he could do the work of two to three men. It hadn't been easy but he'd managed to be both mother and father, too, and now God would take him? Without leaving her with anyone? Surely He could at least provide a decent man, someone suitable to marry.

She was so very tired of thinking about marriage, too.

It was a shame things hadn't worked out with Sinclair Douglas because Ellie had liked him. She hadn't been in love with him, but Sinclair had been easy to like, and she'd felt an almost sisterly affection for him. He was Johanna's big brother after all, and respected by the community. She had confidence in his ability to manage the Burnett Ranch and not squander the resources, or run it into the ground.

She found herself looking at Mr. Baker and then Mr. Fridley. She couldn't imagine either one successfully running the ranch.

Or giving her children. Not that she was ready for children. But one day there would need to be heirs, a boy or girl to inherit her father's land. It was the least she could do to honor his legacy.

A HALF HOUR later the service finally ended, and Ellie exited the church quickly trying to avoid having to speak to either of the two gentlemen, elbowing past parishioners to get to her side.

Stepping outside, she blinked, the overcast day still considerably brighter than the dim church interior, and then spotted Mr. Sheenan parked at the curb, exactly where he promised to be. He hadn't come in a buggy but in the same huge, ugly farm wagon he'd driven to her father's on Wednesday.

Her pace slowed. She winkled her nose, remembering how he'd transported his sheep in the back just a few days ago.

He dropped down from the seat and extended his hand to help her in.

Her gaze swept over him. He was so much taller than she, his shoulders broad in the sturdy brown wool coat, his frame thick with muscle. Perhaps if he'd been built more like Mr. Fridley she wouldn't feel so uneasy. As it was, her skin prickled and her nerves tightened and she drew back a step, thinking this was a bad idea.

"We'll go in my carriage," she said breathlessly, ignoring

his hand, as she battled for a sense of control.

He shrugged lightly. "I won't be driving your carriage."

"No. I will be—"

"You misunderstand, Miss Burnett. You won't be driving me anywhere. Let me assist you in."

"Your wagon is about to fall apart."

"It's not, and I've just scrubbed the seat for you, m'lady." His deep voice with its Irish accent dripped with scorn. "If you're worried about cleanliness, I can assure you that you won't dirty your fine gown on my bench."

Heat rushed through her. Her cheeks grew hot. "Bramble is just a few blocks over. Tie your horse and we can walk."

"I'm not tying my horse, nor walking anywhere, not when hail is forecast for this afternoon. So get in, or let us part ways. I've plenty to do and I'm not strong on patience."

She very nearly told him good day and good riddance but she spied Mr. Baker from the corner of her eye, hustling toward the wagon, his pale brow beaded with perspiration and another film of moisture above his upper lip.

Jaw firming, she lifted her chin and held out her hand, allowing the Irishman to assist her into his wagon.

She settled on the hard wood bench as far from his seat as she could without falling out.

Mr. Sheenan gave her a mocking glance. "Comfortable?"

"Can we just go, please?" she said tightly, hands balling in her lap.

Instead he glanced to the two men standing on the pavement in front of the church. "Should we invite your friends to come along?" he asked sardonically.

Mr. Baker and Mr. Fridley were practically elbowing each other in their haste to reach the wagon. She shook her head. "Sadly, there is no proper bench for them."

"They could ride in the back—"

"Mr. Fridley would be appalled. Perhaps we should move along and get this over with?"

"Couldn't agree more." Mr. Sheenan flicked the reigns and his sturdy horse set off.

It was a short trip down First Avenue, past the triangular shaped Bramble Park with its two saplings and iron bench and then a left on Bramble Lane. There were a dozen houses scattered down Bramble, with two houses on some blocks, and just one house on others. Most of the Victorian homes had been built in the past ten years, some newer than others, but as this was the most prestigious address in Marietta, they were all two to three stories with double hung windows, and columns and porches, and either a tower, turret, or cupola. Some homes were Italianate in design, while others were of the simpler Gothic Revival, and then there were new houses of Queen Anne style.

She looked at each house carefully as they traveled north on Bramble, wondering what it was her father purchased here for her, and if it was a house, or a lot. She'd known for a number of months that her father was up to something, withdrawing money from the local bank for a secret purchase of significant size, but she hadn't expected it to be land on Bramble. She'd thought maybe he was going to build her a new house on their ranch in the valley.

Apparently she'd been wrong.

Her heart sank as Mr. Sheenan slowed and then stopped before a newly built, three story Queen Anne mansion. The wooden shingles on the lower two floors had been painted butter yellow, while the shingles on the third were her favorite ivy green. The thick trim gleamed white, while the tall double hung windows on all three floors promised a bright interior. Her father knew her tastes, though, because the house had a dashing two-story turret and the huge, wrap around porch she'd wanted ever since she was a little girl.

Her father had finally given her the house she'd always dreamed about but instead of it being on their property, beneath the shadow of Emigrant Mountain, it faced majestic Copper Mountain, which wasn't her favorite peak at all.

It was without a doubt a very pretty house, the sparkle of the glass and the soft yellow paint infinitely appealing for a city house, but she didn't want a city house. She would not be living in Marietta. She'd marry and raise her children on the Burnett Ranch in Paradise Valley.

Mr. Sheenan climbed down and reached up to assist her out.

She shook her head. "I don't think so."

"It's impossible to see everything from here," he answered. "The builder gave me the key earlier. He apologized for not having any trees in yet, but I think you'd like the inside. There are gas lines throughout, and each bedroom has its own bath with a proper tub and hot water."

"You've been inside then?"

"I have. It's impressive. My mother would have called it a very fine manor home. High ceilings, a modern kitchen, large windows throughout—"

"That's nice, but I'm not going to live here. My home is in the valley."

"Your house in the valley is primitive compared to this."

She turned her head and looked at him. "Maybe. But would you give up that land—thousands of acres, never mind all that livestock—to live here?"

His gaze narrowed. He studied her a long moment. "No."

"Well, neither will I." She swallowed hard around the lump filling her throat. "Will you please take me back to my carriage now?"

HE SLOWED IN front of the church and then drew his horse to a stop. The wagon rolled a little and then was still.

Ellie clasped her hands together, fingers tightly laced. Her stomach was in knots. The wind had picked up in the past half hour but there was still considerable blue between the gathering clouds. If she left now, she should be able to get home before the storm broke. She ought to go. She shouldn't be desperate, or impulsive. But she'd been desperate ever since her father had told her that his condition was terminal, that there was nothing anyone could do now but try to keep him comfortable.

Ellie's jaw worked. Her eyes burned. "My father approves of you," she said huskily.

"I don't need anyone's approval."

"He'd like me to marry you."

"I know."

She looked at him, throat aching. "Has he spoken to you then about marrying me?"

"He has."

She pressed her gloved fingertips into her palms so hard she could still feel the bite of nail. "And?"

"I came to America to escape family and obligation."

She thought she hated him just then. But she'd hate herself more if she gave up now. Burnett Ranch was worth it. Her pride be damned. "I'm not asking you to like me, and I certainly don't expect you to love me. I just need you to marry me, which will allow me to preserve my father's legacy."

He said nothing and she struggled against the hot rush of anger and shame.

"Is it so impossible to contemplate a life on Burnett Ranch?" she asked tautly.

"It's exceptional property, and one of the finest ranches

in Montana or Wyoming. But I didn't come here to marry—"

"Yes, I understand. You don't want a wife. Well, I don't want a husband, either, but it seems that life is about change and compromise and I'm asking you if you can't please reconsider your position on marriage, and help me save the land I love so much by marrying me." Her voice cracked and her lips quivered and she bit down ruthlessly into her bottom one to hide the fact it was trembling.

For a long moment, there was just the whistle of the icy wind. Perhaps he'd think her eyes were watering from the wind, not shame.

She'd never begged anyone for anything before.

She'd never thought she'd have to beg any man to marry her, either.

"Since you have not yet given me a clear, unequivocal no, let me add that this would be a business arrangement. We would both benefit. You'd be co-owner of one of the biggest, most prosperous ranches in Paradise Valley, and I would have my estate protected."

She held her breath waiting for him to say something, but he didn't.

Ellie pressed on. "We will want children one day to pass the property onto, but I wouldn't expect for us to rush into marital relations, at least not anytime soon. I think we should give ourselves time to get to know each other. I anticipate an adjustment period of six months to a year, something sensible so that we could become familiar with the other—" She broke off, and met his gaze, smile wavering. "I'm not expecting romance. I don't expect much, actually, but if you did agree, and if you agreed marriage could be beneficial, I think it would be wise for us to start out with an agreement in place. Something practical that would lay the framework for the future."

Thomas took all of this in silently. He watched her face as she spoke, letting her words drift over and around him, listening but not listening, thinking it was all rather foolish.

She wanted a husband but no marital relations for six months to a year. She didn't expect romance but desired time for them to become acquainted.

Clearly, she didn't know the difference between men and women.

Nor did she appreciate her desirability.

Men didn't need to know a beautiful woman well to bed her, and Ellie Burnett was beautiful. Even if one didn't like bright fiery red hair, they'd still find her pretty. And back home, Thomas had been known for his soft spot for red-heads. Maybe that was why she'd made such an impression on him, back in December. That hair and those eyes, never mind her full, soft mouth made for long, hot kisses.

"Why me?" he asked when she fell silent again, finally at a loss for words. "Why not Baker or Fridley or any of the other dozen men who have pursued you since Christmas?"

Two spots of color burned high in her cheeks, making

her green eyes glow brighter. Her full pink lips trembled then compressed. "My father approves of you."

"Did he not approve of the others? Did he dislike every single one?"

"No. He wasn't critical of any of them."

"So your father doesn't approve of me, he just doesn't disapprove."

"He's trying to let me choose."

"Which brings us back to my question, why me when you know I don't want you, and I don't want to marry, and I cannot see how I will bring you a minute's joy or happiness—"

"You don't intend to beat me, do you?"

"I don't beat women."

"So why would I be unhappy? You're healthy, ambitious, and, from all appearances, accustomed to hard labor."

Thomas looked at her for a long moment, not sure why he felt like giving her a good shake.

Was she mentally deficit? She knew nothing about him, nor did she seem inclined to find out anything important about him. She wasn't even asking the right questions. Instead, it was enough for her that he was young and physically fit. "I can ride and work late, rounding up cattle or harvesting a field, but there will be plenty of nights where weather or illness will keep us trapped in the house together. Don't you think you should know more about the man you marry than if he can carry heavy things?"

Her brow lifted. "Should I interview you, then? Or write to someone, requesting references? Or, maybe, you have those references on your person, which would be wonderful since time is of the essence."

"Did anyone ever tell you sarcasm is unattractive in a lady?"

"I try not to spend a lot of time worrying about what people think of me. I know who I am, and I know what I want, and I'm determined to keep my father's land, and pass it on to my children. And maybe I'm not the simpering sort of lady you prefer—you can blame my father for that—but my instincts are good and they tell me if I want Burnett Ranch to survive for the next generation, you'd be the one to help me do it."

Her voice deepened and her eyes shone but she never looked away from his gaze. "If my instincts are wrong, tell me. But I think you wouldn't just keep the property intact, but you'd love it the way the land needs to be loved."

She was a puzzle. Spoiled to a fault, high-handed, and sharp-tongued, she was also heartbreakingly loyal to her father and she would suffer when he died.

"Where is your mother?" he asked bluntly.

"She died when I was five."

"No brothers or sisters?"

"She died in childbirth."

He looked away, not wanting to care, not wanting to be concerned, but he was concerned. "Aunts, uncles, grandparents?" he asked gruffly.

"Maybe in Texas. Or Massachusetts. My mama was born in Boston." Her slim shoulders shifted. "But I've never met any relations. Apparently there was a falling out years ago when Mama married Papa."

So she would be alone. And she would grieve and her grief would be made worse because there was no one else.

He looked away, frustrated. "You need to marry someone who will be kind to you, and patient. I am neither kind, nor patient—"

"I'm not looking for a girlfriend. I have Miss Douglas for gossip and girlish confidences—"

"You say that because you've been sheltered. Not all men are the same—"

"Exactly. I don't want a gentrified man from the city. I don't care about etiquette. I don't need a dance partner. I need a husband who won't be afraid of blisters and hard work, a husband who isn't frightened by the howl of wolves and willing to rescue the stray calf even in the middle of a storm. If that is you, I want to marry you. If that is not you, then tell me, and I will continue my search and respect you for not wasting my time."

He was not tempted, and the only thing he felt was irritation. He didn't need people, or entanglements, and this woman with her gleaming red hair and wide, bright eyes would be nothing but trouble. He'd left Rathkeale to get away from complications and he liked Montana. He was beginning to settle in here in Paradise Valley. It almost felt comfortable, but it wouldn't be comfortable with her around.

In fact, just sitting next to her in this damn wagon made him exceedingly uncomfortable. His trousers were too tight now and his body felt thick and hard, his pulse quick, his temper stirring.

"Was there never a suitable groom?" he asked shortly, wanting nothing more than to drop her off at the church and be done with her.

So why didn't he just end this miserable conversation?

Why didn't he just leave her to her fate?

He didn't care.

He *didn't* care.

He didn't want to care.

But, as the silence stretched, and he could see how she struggled with words, color coming and going, washing her pale cheeks with red before fading again, he felt tense and impatient with the men of Marietta who should have wanted her, men who wanted wives and babies and stability. Men who needed anchors and partners.

He was not one of them.

"There was someone," she said faintly. "We were briefly engaged, but he loved another." Her smooth jaw firmed, expression cool. "I wouldn't have allowed the courtship to proceed so slowly if I'd known he wasn't going to marry me. Now there is no time for anything but exchanging vows."

"I understand the urgency. You are being practical. But I had sisters. Girls are not boys, women are not men. You can't possibly expect me to believe there is nothing you want for yourself."

"Before my father became ill, I had dreams, but what is the point of dreaming when your heart is breaking?" She looked at him and suddenly her guard was down and he could see in her eyes her despair. She was hollow and scared.

"I want my father to live," she said. "And I'd give everything up—the land, the livestock, the income—just to have another year with him. But God's not listening and so here we are. I'm not good at begging. I don't have a lot of experience pleading, but if I need to—"

"No." He cut her off swiftly, brutally, unable to stomach anymore.

He hated grief. He had no use for emotions, good or bad. Work made sense. He understood blood and sweat. And sex. But that was all. Because that was all he had left. Whoever he'd been before was gone, buried with his family in County Limerick.

"I can't give you tenderness, but I'm not afraid of wolves or bears or banshees—"

"Banshees," she interrupted with a gurgle of tearful laughter. "My mother was always warning me of the banshees. Hooligans and banshees." She reached up and swiped the tears before they could fall. "It's good to know you're not afraid of fairies or mischief makers."

"How can I, when I was one myself?"

"Not a fairy, I hope."

"No, but I did get into my share of trouble as a boy, and I suffered the consequences. I don't look for trouble anymore, but if there's something that needs to be done, I'll do it." He looked into her eyes, held her gaze. "But know, if we do this, you won't be playing lady of the manor. You'll be expected to do your share, and there won't be anyone to wait on you hand and foot."

"No one waits on me now." She hesitated, her expressive face revealing her uncertainty as well as hope. "So… is that a yes?"

He wanted to say no. He wanted to walk away but, God help him, he couldn't. "I need to speak to your father first."

"To ask for his permission to marry me? If that is the case, it's not necessary. He'll say yes because at this point, it's merely a formality—"

"Not to me."

"When would you approach him?"

He hated this, all of this, but something in him couldn't allow her to lose everything. He couldn't save her father, but he could save her land. He understood the land because he understood sun and rain and the cycle of life. He could make something of the ranch.

She was another matter.

"I'll call on him late this afternoon," he said grimly. "And we'll see what happens then."

CHAPTER FOUR

ELLIE WAS IN her second-floor bedroom trying on her Easter dress with Johanna when her father rang the little bell he kept next to his armchair, the bell only used when he needed her.

Ellie slipped out of the pale coral dress and into a simple gingham cotton dress before hurrying downstairs to check on her father. She stopped short in the doorway when she spotted the Irishman in the front parlor standing before the fire. She hadn't heard him arrive, and hadn't realized he was in the house, closeted with her father.

"Oh!" She blinked, suddenly breathless from the rush of emotions—surprise, anxiety, excitement. She pressed her hands against her skirts to hide her nervousness. "You did come."

"I said I would," he answered, his gaze moving slowly over her, taking in every inch from the top of her head to the hem of her skirt.

She flushed beneath the inspection. This was new. He'd never looked at her quite so intently, or possessively. It was almost as if he was examining an expensive purchase, checking for flaws in the merchandise.

Uncomfortable, Ellie glanced to her father in his winged chair. Her father's shoulders were slumped and yet his eyes were bright, even over bright. She wasn't sure if that was a good sign or a bad sign.

"Well?" she asked, struggling to hide her impatience.

"I've given my blessing, if you can be persuaded," her father said. "I've told Mr. Sheenan I'm not sure you can be persuaded. After all, you've said no to a half dozen proposals by men with far more than what he has to offer."

They were both looking at her now, Mr. Sheenan's expression sardonic, her father's heavy-lidded and inscrutable.

"I suppose she can't answer," Mr. Sheenan said, breaking the awkward silence, "if she hasn't been asked." He left his position at the hearth and crossed the room in a few long strides.

In front of her, he extended his hand, palm up. She glanced down at his hand, large, calloused, strong, and then up into his face. His dark eyes glinted at her, and she wondered if he would kneel and formally propose. Reluctantly she placed her hand in his. His skin was warm, the palm dry and firm.

His fingers curled around hers. "Miss Burnett, would you do me the honor of being my wife?"

There was no kneeling proposal. No tenderness. Nothing remotely romantic—which was good—because she hadn't wanted romance.

This was a business agreement. She was getting what she wanted—the ranch. And he was getting what he wanted—wealth.

They didn't have to like each other, or have feelings for the other. They were strangers, and they'd remain strangers for a long time to come.

"Yes," she answered, her voice low but firm. "I will."

JOHANNA WAS WAITING for Ellie at the top of the staircase, eyes wide, mouth gaping. "Did that really just happen?"

Ellie blushed and allowed herself to be pulled back toward the privacy of her bedroom. "Did what just happen?"

"The marriage proposal. And you accepted, didn't you?"

"You were eavesdropping!"

"Of course I was, once I realized it was Thomas Sheenan calling on you." Johanna closed the bedroom door firmly and put her hands on her hips. "I can't believe you're seriously considering—"

"Not considering, I accepted his proposal, and I'm marrying him. Now let's finish the fitting—"

"Do you know anything about him? He's considered to be very mysterious. Sinclair said he's been in Crawford County for months and hasn't tried to make any friends."

"Maybe he's too busy working to socialize."

"Maybe he has something to hide."

"Like what?"

"I don't know, but is he really the man you want to marry?"

Caught off guard, Ellie stiffened. "I'm not in a position to be choosy at this point, and he's certainly better than Mr. Baker or Mr. Fridley!"

"Well, I thought Mr. Fridley could be charming at times, and Mr. Baker wasn't handsome but he was rather sweet."

"And dull."

"But at least manageable, and Mr. Sheenan is not going to be manageable. He's going to be a problem—"

"You don't know that."

"I do! Just look at him. He's not like any of the men who are from around here. He reminds me of the men who worked in the mines in Butte, the ones from Dublin Gulch. They were rough and hard and they didn't make good husbands."

Ellie turned away, moving to the bed where her Easter dress was spread out. "I think we should change the subject."

"Don't be upset with me, Ellie. I'm trying to be a good friend."

"I appreciate that. I do." She ran her fingers over the elegant skirt and delicate tulle on the bodice. "But I'm not going to wear this for Easter," she said quietly. "I'm going to save it for my wedding. I'll be getting married just after Easter and there's no time to make me a wedding dress. My Easter dress will be more than adequate—"

"Now you're just being mean. You must have a proper

wedding gown! White or cream silk. Very elegant, very fashionable, just as if you were in New York—"

"Oh, Johanna, I don't care about New York. The fashions and customs of the East Coast have never interested me."

"But they interest most ladies here, and people look to you, and they all know I dress you."

"So this is about you. I'm to be your advertisement."

"You've always been. Why do you think I have so many customers now? You make my clothes beautiful. Everyone wants to be as elegant and stylish as you, which is why you're not wearing your Easter dress."

"Does my dress look like everyone else's?"

"Of course not. This year everyone is wearing lavender and violet. During the parade you'll see violet with blue, or violet with green, or a ruffled cape in violet over a dress that is robin egg blue."

"My gown is pink—"

"Pale coral."

"So it could serve as a wedding gown."

"No, it can't. You must wear white."

"I'll never be able to wear it again."

"And when has that ever bothered you? Your wardrobe is filled with things you've only worn once."

"But can you do it in time? Because, honestly, Johanna, I need more than a jacket. My father would not approve of me walking down the aisle in a jacket and petticoats."

"You'll be properly, and beautifully covered. I promise. Now let's put your Easter dress on one more time and let me check the hem and we're done."

Ellie stepped from her gingham into the pale coral confection with the pink and coral and cream braid. It was a mouthwatering dress, like one of those delicious ices she'd had when she'd visited the pleasure gardens in Butte last summer.

Johanna helped ease the dress up over her shoulders and began fastening the back. "This is gorgeous on you," she murmured. "I'm so envious of your little waist. You don't even need a corset."

"And I envy you for your curves. I'm built like a boy."

"Not so. I've dressed girls who are built like boys. You are not one of them. Now hold still and let me check the hem all the way around."

It wasn't easy but Ellie managed to keep still while Johanna tugged and measured and slipped a stitch here and there. "I think we're done," Johanna said at last.

"Good! Because you're supposed to be at your brother's for supper and if you don't leave soon you won't get there until after dark and he won't like that."

"You're trying to get rid of me."

"Yes, I am, because I don't want Sinclair angry with you, and I'm anxious to speak to my father and see what he thinks of all this."

Johanna unfastened the hooks and laces and eased the

gown off Ellie's shoulders. "I just think it's awfully presumptuous for Mr. Sheenan to approach you. He's virtually penniless—"

"I approached him." Ellie stepped from the gown and reached for her gingham dress. "And I actually proposed to him, first. It wasn't a pretty proposal, either. I practically had to beg him to marry me. He doesn't like me. I don't like him, either, but he's better than Fridley or Baker. Neither of them would know what to do with the ranch, and Mr. Sheenan will."

"And will Mr. Sheenan know what to do with you?"

"It's not going to be that kind of marriage—"

"Oh, Ellie. Marriage is marriage. There's no escaping certain duties and responsibilities." Johanna's gaze met Ellie's in the looking glass as she gave the new dress a shake. "If you know what I mean."

"I do, and we're not going to... to... jump... right into that side of marriage. We've agreed to take our time, and get acquainted."

"Very gentlemanly of him. But can you trust him? What do you know about him?"

"He's Irish. He looks to be late twenties. He seems strong and healthy. He has a big frame, experience with livestock, he'll be able to handle the physical labor."

"Those are your only qualifications for a husband?"

"The ranch is a lot of work. The days are quite long."

Johanna grimaced. "What about his brain? Or do you

not care?"

"I don't think he's a dumb ox, but I'm not worried about his intelligence. I'll be the one making the decisions. His job will be to carry them out."

"And does he know this?"

"He will."

"You'll tell him just that… that you're in charge?"

Ellie lifted a shoulder. "It is my ranch. And it falls to me to make sure it succeeds."

Johanna sighed. "I don't think you understand marriage, Ellie, or the nature of men—"

"I have been surrounded by men my entire life. I understand them well enough."

"If you want to manage a man, marry Mr. Baker. I'm not sure this Irishman—"

"Thomas Sheenan."

"Mr. Sheenan is as you describe, he might not appreciate you managing him. Most men do not welcome an interfering female."

"Interfering female? It's my ranch! He's lucky to marry me. I'm sure he's counting his lucky stars at this very moment."

"I wouldn't tell him that. It will only be a thorn in his side, and a source of conflict. I know, because it was very difficult for Sinclair and McKenna. When they first fell in love, she was a copper heiress, and he just a miner. The disparity in position was impossible. Sin never felt worthy of

her until he'd succeeded on his own. But by marrying you
soon, Mr. Sheenan will have had no chance to prove himself,
or to succeed on his own. I'm afraid he'll always resent you
for that, and you won't respect him the way a man wants to
be respected—"

"You've never had a date, Johanna! I don't know what
makes you such an expert on men."

"I listen to my clients. I'm surround by women. I have a
pretty good idea of what makes a relationship work, and it's
not being unevenly yoked."

"This is becomingly appallingly somber and biblical. We
will be fine."

"I just think you need to have a care. Your Mr. Sheenan
was raised in Ireland, not here. He might have very different
ideas about women taking charge."

"Well, I'm not going to tiptoe around him, and I wasn't
raised me to be one of those silent, deferential ladies. Papa
taught me to have confidence, and I do. Now stop fussing
and get to your brother's before he comes looking for you!"

An hour later, when Ellie recounted her conversation
with Johanna to her father, she expected him to smile, or be
mildly amused. Instead he sighed.

"She's right, your Miss Douglas," he said heavily. "You
need to proceed carefully, Ellie. No man desires an opinion-
ated bride."

"You always let me have an opinion."

"Because you were my daughter, not my wife."

"Why is it different?"

"It just is."

"It doesn't make sense to me."

He gave her a long, penetrating look before tipping his head back against the chair, eyes closing.

Ellie watched him, aware that he was far too gray, and while he'd always had strong, high cheekbones, his cheeks were now hollowed out, the bones brutally prominent. He was beyond gaunt, closer to skeletal.

"Let's not discuss this anymore," she said, going to his side and adjusting his blanket, drawing it higher on his chest and tucking it in around him. "I thought you'd be amused. I didn't intend to worry you."

"But I am worried. I'm afraid I've failed you."

"Failed me how? You've been the best father, the most loving father—"

"But I've shielded you from reality, and I'm afraid you're going to be hurt, badly hurt." His eyes opened and he looked into hers. "You don't have to marry Sheenan. Take the house on Bramble—"

"I don't *want* the house on Bramble. I want to stay here, in our home."

"But this isn't the life I wanted you to have. This isn't why I worked so hard." His voice rasped, and then he inhaled sharply, setting off a spasm of coughing.

She waited for the coughing to end. It seemed like forever. After a while, she had to look away from his face, and how difficult it was for him to catch his breath. He was dying in front of her and there was nothing she could do.

When he was finally quiet, she pulled the rocking chair next to him and sat down, taking his hand in hers. "Papa, you *have* worked hard. This ranch is your legacy. There's no way I can just let it go, or allow it to disappear. It's your land, *our* land, and it ties us together. This land will be our bond even after you are gone. Think about it. It's all I will have of you, and it's how I will remember you. Can't you see it's worth fighting for?"

His eyes watered. "But, Ellie, in the end it is just land. Acreage. Dirt and weeds. Heads of cattle. And you will remember me. I know you will remember me. The land isn't essential."

"You're wrong. I know you because of the land, and how you've worked it, first in Texas, and then on those endless cattle drives, and now here. This ranch is your life's work. It's thirty years!"

"You're not even twenty-two—"

"Exactly. Young and healthy and determined to preserve your property. *Our* property. And in my heart I know you will be pleased, as well as grateful, that your legacy lives on."

He was silent and Ellie battled her temper. "Papa, if I was a man, we wouldn't even be having this conversation." Frustration deepened her voice, making it crack. "It would be assumed that I would take over, and do everything in my power to ensure the ranch's success. And instead of arguing with me about moving into a new house on Bramble, you'd be spending your last few months teaching me everything you knew about managing this place. You'd ride with me across the property and share with me wisdom, advice, encouragement. Instead you've done everything you can to discourage me—"

"For your good."

She laughed. "Then you don't know me, Papa—"

"Ah, but I do. You were meant for a city and a big mansion and lots of staff to ensure that you are comfortable and happy. You love your comforts, Ellie. You love your fine buggy, your new dresses, and pocket money to spend. Just because I preferred the open land, doesn't mean it's your future."

"Yes, I'd like a fancy house, as you put it. But I can have that fine house here on our land. I don't need to live in Marietta, and I certainly don't want to be shoulder to shoulder with townspeople, which is why I'm getting married. And you like Mr. Sheenan. You told me so. You wanted him for me—"

"I never said such a thing."

"But you asked me, quite pointedly, why I wouldn't consider him. I know you approve of him, so give me your support and help me decide when this wedding should be and where it will be. What do you think of the Graff?"

"If that's what you want."

"How many people? Who should we invite?"

"You handle the details. Just tell me when and where to show up."

She smiled. "I can do that."

IN THE END, the wedding was not to be the brief, but elegant Wednesday ceremony at the Graff, but a rushed exchanging of vows in the Burnett front parlor Saturday noon in the Easter dress since the wedding gown wasn't finished. Ellie wasn't complaining, though. How could she, when just yesterday, on Good Friday, she hadn't thought her father would last the night?

Alone in her room, Ellie gathered her long thick hair, rolling and pinning the red mass into the full, feminine style her father preferred. It took patience, as well as many sections and pins to create the vivid auburn crown but eventually it was secure. Gently she teased a few loose curls free to frame her face and neck before pinning her mother's long, delicate lace veil to her chignon.

The veil had a small tear where she'd torn it as a little girl after discovering it tucked in the cedar chest at the foot of her parents' bed, but the tear made the veil all the more dear. Her eyes stung as she then attached her mother's pearl earrings, one lobe and then the other. It had been a long time since she'd thought of her mother, but suddenly Ellie missed her almost desperately, thinking she should be there with her, helping her dress.

But no, it wouldn't do to cry for her mama. Today would be happy. Today she was getting married.

Blinking hard, she turned to look out the window, her gaze taking in the stable and barn and all the land beyond. She loved the ranch, and the mountains, and the dark blue Yellowstone River winding through the valley floor. In summer, the valley glimmered blues and greens. In autumn, it turned bronze and gold. Winter and spring the gold faded, the wan yellow dusted white. This was her valley, her home, not tidy little Marietta with its handsome courthouse and two-story library, courtesy of money from the Frasier copper mine. She wasn't a Frasier and she didn't want to be part of a town that the Frasier money built. No, this swathe of land beneath Emigrant Peak was hers, this was where she belonged, and maybe she'd always imagined her wedding at St. James with a reception at the Graff Hotel, but in the end, this was probably the best wedding for her.

A wedding at home. A small, private affair in front of the parlor hearth. Instead of a minister, the clerk from Marietta's city hall would officiate, and he'd arrived a half hour ago and was waiting in the parlor.

The only guests would be the Douglas family, and she could spot Sinclair Douglas's buggy in the distance, the smart, modern carriage drawn by a team of grays.

Now all they needed was the groom himself, Mr. Thomas Sheenan. She wasn't worried, though. He wasn't late yet, and she was certain he'd come. He might not want her, but how did one refuse a gift like the Burnett Ranch?

Ellie sat back down on the small upholstered stool before her French dressing table, the set a gift from her father for her eighteenth birthday. She gazed in the mirror, not recognizing the woman with the veil and pearls. Maybe it was because the woman in the mirror looked uncertain and scared.

Ellie closed her eyes and drew a deep breath, and tried again, opening her eyes to look at herself once more. Green eyes. Small nose. Wide mouth.

She forced a smile. But the expression in her eyes was still empty. Sad.

She smiled harder, lifting her chin, and then tears filled her eyes and she covered her face, not wanting to look anymore.

She would do this, and she'd make her father proud but, oh, it wasn't as easy as she'd imagined.

But what were the alternatives? There were none. She had no options at this point, and so she'd give her father this day, a perfect day. Perfect, in this instance, being peace of mind. He'd be here to witness the marriage, and know that once he was gone, she wouldn't be alone.

The knock on the door made her turn from the mirror.

"Come in," she called, expecting Johanna. Instead it was Thomas Sheenan filling the doorway, tall, broad-shouldered, and oh so very intimidating in a formal black coat, black vest, white pleated shirt and bow tie. She wondered who had loaned him the suit because surely it wasn't from his own closet. Either way, he appeared a proper groom, with not even a hair out of place. "Mr. Sheenan, you look very fine today."

His head inclined, his set jaw easing a fraction. "As do you."

He sounded sincere, and suddenly there was a lump in her throat and her eyes burned. "Thank you. And thank you for dropping everything to marry today. I know it's been quite hectic, even a little havey-cavey, but I appreciate you being here so that we could hold the service now, instead of next week."

"Yesterday must have been a difficult day."

"It was frightening, yes, but Papa is here today and I can't ask for more than that."

"You could, but I don't suppose you would."

She didn't even try to puzzle out his meaning. It was enough that he'd agreed to marry her and he was here and her father was here. It was a miracle really. "I'm content."

"So, no second thoughts?"

"No. What about you? Are you having cold feet?"

His dark gaze met hers, searching her eyes for who knew what. "It wouldn't be fair of me to do that to you."

"True." She drew a quick, sharp breath, suddenly filled with butterflies. "How have you left things with Mr. Gilmore? Does he expect you back, or are you free?"

"I've left his employ. This morning I finished moving the

last of my things out."

"Where are your things now?"

"Here."

She swallowed against the rise of nausea. She shouldn't be surprised. They were marrying, so he'd live here, of course. She'd known he'd be moving in to the house, but it was all happening so quickly now.

"Your father directed me to store everything in the attic and, for now, I'll be sleeping in the guest room at the end of the hall."

For now. The words sent a shiver of sensation through her. It wasn't a comfortable sensation and her pulse quickened. *Don't think about it.* Don't think about anything but securing the ranch and making Papa happy.

"I know that room is small," she said, struggling for a normalcy she didn't feel. "But I hope it will be adequate."

"I'm not worried about the size of the room. The bed is another matter. It's quite short."

"It was once the nursery."

"That would explain the cot-sized mattress."

"I'm sure we can get a larger bed for the room. I understand that the mercantile in Marietta carries good mattresses."

"I'll sort it out. Don't worry about it. You have enough on your mind."

She nodded, grateful, even as a rush of adrenaline made her increasingly queasy. This marriage to Thomas Sheenan was really happening. He'd already moved into the house. They were discussing beds and mattresses and soon he'd be sleeping just a few feet from her.

The butterflies in her middle intensified. Ellie pressed a hand to her stomach trying to calm her nerves but her pulse was racing faster, not slower, and she suddenly wanted to throw up.

"You're looking pale," he said.

She struggled to smile but hot gritty tears stung the back of her eyes. "I'm fine. Just a little bit overwrought, but that's to be expected as I didn't sleep more than an hour or two last night. I was afraid to leave my father's side. Yesterday was so frightening. I thought he was gone for certain at one point and I must have screamed, loudly, because Mrs. Baxter and Mr. Harrison and Johnny, they all came running." She knew she was babbling, but she couldn't stop the words, they spilled from her in a tremulous breathless stream. Even her voice was pitched higher than normal but she was afraid to draw a deep breath, fearful she'd burst into tears. "But he's here today, so that's something to celebrate."

"And our marriage today. Something else to celebrate."

She looked away, unable to meet the Irishman's dark penetrating gaze. "Mrs. Baxter made us a cake. I haven't seen it, yet."

"It's on the dining table now. It's quite impressive, considering she had so little time to prepare."

"Mrs. Baxter is an excellent baker. My father loves her

scones. He says they are nearly as good as his mother's, and apparently those were the best he's ever tasted." Ellie mentally kicked herself, not sure why she'd said any of that. She felt as if she was losing control, her thoughts as wild as her pulse.

Knotting her hands in her lap, she looked to the door, and then the window, not knowing what to focus on. She just knew she couldn't look at Mr. Sheenan. He made her uneasy. He wasn't like the men her father employed. Nor was he like the men she'd dated. Sinclair Douglas was big and muscular, but Sinclair had a way of putting others at ease. He had the manners of a gentleman, as well as kindness in his eyes. There was nothing kind in Thomas Sheenan's gaze. No, his gaze was dark and hard and far too intense.

He reminded her of a wild horse trapped in a corral, just waiting for the chance to escape. Break free.

He wouldn't be easy to manage.

It would be strange living with such a man. She couldn't imagine ever sleeping with such a man. It was difficult just thinking that he'd be down the hall in the guest room, never mind one day sharing her bed.

But that was down the road, she hastily reminded herself. Months and months from now. She wouldn't even think about the physical side of marriage for a year. Instead, she'd focus on becoming acquainted. She didn't expect friendship from him, nor affection. But affection was not necessary. As long as he respected her, she'd be fine. They'd be fine. The goal was for them to be able to work together. Cooperation would be essential.

And just like that she became aware of how he filled the entire doorway, as if a wall, not a door and her heart gave another hard, sickening thump.

Her father had told her that men were a lot like livestock. They needed regular feeding, and water, and sleep. They didn't do well when hungry. They could be grumpy when tired. But provide a man a good meal, and a good bed, and he'd be content.

She drew a slow painful breath. She was counting on that, at least.

His dark gaze narrowed as he studied her. "Do you have any questions you want to ask me? Is there anything you'd like to know before we go downstairs?"

There were a hundred things she wanted to know about him but not one coherent question came to mind. It was impossible to think when panic thumped through her veins, making her throat thicken and her stomach churn.

Stalling for time, she turned back to the mirror and inspected her hair, and reached for a pin. "Have you invited anyone to join us today?"

"*That* is your question?" His voice sharpened, the Irish accent growing pronounced.

She flinched a little, feeling far too sensitive. Her hand shook as she slid the pin into her coiled hair. She reached for another, and added that to the heavy mass of curls at the back. "I just wondered if you'd have any family with us."

"No."

"Do you have family in America?"

"I had an uncle, but he died shortly after I arrived, before I had the chance to see him."

"Where did he live?"

"Bozeman."

"That's why you came to Montana?" she asked, striving to sound calm, hoping to be properly conversational as their gaze met in the reflection.

But his answer was curt. "No."

Clearly this wasn't the conversation he wanted to be having with her. "Since none of my questions seem to be making you happy, tell me what I should be asking you, Mr. Sheenan."

He practically scowled at her from the doorway. "I don't know. I've never been married before."

"Excellent. That makes two of us," she said lightly to hide her sudden terror.

Thomas Sheenan was scaring her half to death. Dressed in a fine coat with a smart vest and bow tie, he should have appeared elegant, and polished. Civilized. Instead he looked like a wild animal smashed into a tailored suit.

His shoulders were too wide. He was too tall, the top of his head nearly touching the doorframe. He dwarfed the doorway, and these were not small doorways, either. Her father had built everything oversized to accommodate his height. Her father, a tall, tough Texan had always made her feel protected, and safe.

But Thomas Sheenan did not make her feel safe, not when the chiseled planes of his face looked granite hard, and his dark gaze burned her through the looking glass.

He was angry. He resented her.

"You'd hoped I'd changed my mind, though," she said suddenly, realizing why he'd come to her room, understanding now his tension.

He didn't want to be the one to break things off, but he'd hoped she would. He'd hoped she'd release him from their arrangement.

A dozen men had flung themselves at her feet, wanting her, wanting her property and wealth, but she'd chosen a man who didn't want her.

Just as Sinclair Douglas hadn't wanted her.

But he'd never been rude about it, and he'd broken their engagement because he loved another.

Ellie felt a sharp prickle in her skin, awareness making the fine hair rise at her nape and across her arms. Her gaze locked with his and she leaned on her elbows, needing the dressing table for support. "Do you love another?"

"No."

"You're not promised to another woman?"

"If I were, I wouldn't be standing here."

"But you don't want to be standing here, do you?"

"No."

She told herself not to be hurt. There had to have been

more reluctant husbands in the past. She was sure if she looked through the pages of history, she'd discover that there were other men who did not embrace marriage and fatherhood. She was sure there were others who'd view it as not just unappealing, but a chore.

"At least we can be honest with each other," she said coolly. "That is something we can celebrate today as we cut Mrs. Baxter's cake."

His brow lowered. "It's not too late to choose a different groom. I saw Fridley in town last night. He'd be here in an hour if you sent word."

She rose and let her full skirts fall before giving him a small, mocking smile. "Alas, I have chosen you, and here I am, dressed and ready, eager to be your wife."

His eyes narrowed, thick black lashes dropping, concealing his expression but not before she caught a bright hard glitter in the brown irises. "You are committed to your plan."

"Our plan," she corrected. "Just as this is to be our life here."

"You say that now, Miss Burnett, but I doubt you'll feel that way later."

"Why? This marriage protects my inheritance. I should be grateful to you, just as I am sure you are grateful to me for the opportunity..." Her voice faded as his face remained expressionless and he made no effort to agree with her. "This is good for both of us. It's not one-sided."

"But it won't be the same for you after we marry. Your

life won't be the same—"

"Because my father will be gone?" She shrugged, unable to hide her irritation. Must he be so gloomy about everything today? "I'm aware that life is about to change. I'll have to adapt. You'll have to adapt. It will take time, and we have time. There is no urgency that I can see."

He didn't answer, and the silence became increasingly heavy and surprisingly intimate. She squirmed inwardly as the silence wrapped around them, binding them together there, making her aware of how small her bedroom was, and yet how large her bed was for such a small space.

She swallowed hard. "You have promised to give me time," she added firmly, even though her legs shook beneath her. "There's to be no rush to consummate the marriage, or make significant changes. Mr. Harrison has worked with my father from almost the beginning and knows this property inside out. He's competent and trustworthy and he can manage the ranch while you become acquainted with the land and livestock."

"When we marry, Harrison will work for me, not the other way around."

"Of course with time—"

"I've already spoken with Harrison. He understands his position, and mine."

Her brow furrowed. "You've already spoken to him? Without my father's permission?"

"Your father arranged the meeting. Everyone is aware

that there will be change. And it's not going to be easy, not in the beginning, not for anyone, but especially not for you."

His words, coupled with his tone, made her mouth dry and her stomach heave. She wanted to sit down. Wanted to lie down and grab a pillow and scream until she was hoarse and unable to make another sound.

Instead, she smiled, squaring her shoulders, smashing the panic, reminding herself she was a Burnett. She was her father's daughter. She could do this.

"I think that just about covers everything." Her voice lilted. Her smile curved her lips. She would do this. "When you go downstairs, will you please send Miss Douglas up?"

He looked at her for a long, discomfiting moment, his brown eyes searching for something, she knew not what, but she let him look, and look until he'd had his fill. Apparently satisfied, his dark head inclined and he turned around, and walked away, leaving her even more unsettled than she'd been before.

Unsettled and angry, because he made her feel as if he was doing her a huge favor, and she didn't like it.

He should be grateful for this marriage. He should be dancing down the hall, whistling a merry tune.

She wasn't homely. She had all her teeth and they were straight and healthy, and white. Her eyes weren't crossed. Her skin wasn't pockmarked. She was slim with just the right amount of bust and hips not to be mistaken for a boy. Her hair was gorgeous. It was her best feature, although her father had told her she had good eyes, too.

But most importantly, she was rich. Incredibly rich.

Thomas Sheenan was lucky. He should be counting his blessings right now. He should be on his knees, thanking the good Lord, but somehow, as his heavy footsteps receded, she doubted it.

THOMAS WALKED DOWN the hall, away from the bedroom to the stairs, jaw clenched so hard his teeth ached. He did not come to America to marry, or to fall in step with someone's grand plan.

While he liked Archibald Burnett well enough, Thomas didn't feel beholden to him in any way, nor was he awed by the old Texan's legacy. He understood that Miss Burnett was fiercely proud of her father, but Thomas left Ireland to escape heritage and tradition. He'd left Ireland to become someone else.

Montana's Paradise Valley was nothing like County Limerick, and he embraced Montana's long, treacherous winters and very short summers. He embraced the hardship and the challenge. He didn't want it easy. He wanted to fight to survive. He wanted the struggle, because then, and only then, did he feel.

Marrying Ellie made it all too easy. The huge, successful ranch. The wealth. The beautiful, young woman with the bright copper hair and dancing eyes not just dangled before him, but dropped into his lap. He didn't have to do anything but say a few words today—utter the simple vows—and he'd become shockingly wealthy. He'd have more than he could have ever dreamed, with no effort on his part.

He'd be set for life... no sweat, muscle, or thought required.

It made him slightly nauseous. And yet, no one had put a gun to his head. He didn't have to say yes to her. He didn't have to be moved by the old man's plea. Thomas could have refused both. He probably should have refused both, but the old man was dying and his daughter had no one and it was hell to be left alone in the world, with everyone she'd ever loved in the ground. Gone.

He knew because everyone he'd ever loved was gone, too.

Which was why he'd left Rathkeale. He needed to get away from the past, and memories of his family, and his sister, Eliza, the last of them, whispering in her final weeks, *"Forgive me. I hate to be a burden..."*

She wasn't a burden. None of them had been a burden. But, after burying her, he'd vowed he was done with family. Done with ties and commitments. He wanted to avoid people and entanglements, particularly emotional entanglements, and yet, here he was, minutes away from marrying a woman who would soon have her world turned upside down.

Dear God, but he was the wrong man for the job.

He should have refused the Burnetts. He should have

just walked away. He didn't owe them anything. They didn't need to know that he was numb on the inside. Cold. Dead.

Even he knew that dead men did not make good husbands. Dead men were not good for much of anything, and yet, here he was, about to commit to a woman who would soon need someone strong, and loyal, and able to give meaning to her shattered life.

CHAPTER FIVE

THE WEDDING WAS mercifully brief.

The only guests were the four Douglasses—Johanna, Sinclair, McKenna, and Mrs. Douglas—and Mr. Harrison, the Burnett Ranch manager.

Her father didn't stand for the brief ceremony, too weak to do anything but give his consent from his chair by the fire.

Ellie barely looked at her groom, her focus on her father whose labored breathing signaled the beginning of the end.

She clutched the small bouquet of lilies that Johanna had borrowed from the lavish Easter decorations at St. James in Marietta. Her hands were damp where she gripped the velvet wrapped stems so tightly.

And then it was done. Thomas Sheenan was lifting her veil and he bent down to place a kiss on the corner of her mouth. It was chaste and sweet and she hoped it made her father happy.

There were hugs afterward, and tears, when she crouched next to her father to whisper, "Happy, Papa?"

"Yes," he rasped. "You are even more beautiful than your mama."

She almost fell apart then, but was saved from disgrace by the loud pop of champagne as Sinclair opened the first of the two bottles he'd brought for the reception.

Sinclair toasted the new couple, and then Mrs. Baxter called them to the table where they were served a formal four course meal, prepared by Mrs. Baxter and her oldest daughter Mae.

There were more toasts during dinner, and conversation and laughter, although Ellie wasn't sure who was laughing since it wasn't her or Mr. Sheenan. Mr. Sheenan said virtually nothing throughout the meal, his expression grim.

Ellie glanced down at her hand at one point, her attention caught by the simple ring on her fourth finger. It was a gold band, neither wide nor heavy, and every time she looked at it, her heart stuttered and fell.

She was married. *Married.* Mrs. Thomas Sheenan, too. She didn't hate the name, but it didn't feel like her name. It didn't feel like her. But that didn't stop Johanna from repeatedly using her new name to get her attention.

Mrs. Sheenan, would you like another dinner roll?

Mrs. Sheenan, do you need something to drink?

Mrs. Sheenan…

Ellie smiled each time, aware that Johanna was teasing her, but the game wore on her as the meal went on, making her raw, each reference to the new surname reminding her that she no longer belonged to her father, but to this brooding, black-haired, dark-eyed stranger.

Her eyes burned as she looked at her father, stooped over in his chair. She'd hoped after the ceremony he'd go to bed, but he'd refused, determined to be at the table, determined to be the proper host, even though he could barely hold himself upright.

Her proud, foolish papa. He ought to be in bed, resting, not entertaining, but she understood that for him this was a momentous day. His only child was marrying. His Ellie had become a woman. A wife.

Her lips quivered as she drank him in. The snowy beard, the impressive moustache, the Texas heart beating in his chest.

TWO HOURS LATER, everyone departed and Thomas and Mr. Harrison helped her father upstairs to his bedroom, and then helped him change, before putting him to bed.

But once in his nightshirt, tucked into the big bed with the handsome walnut headboard, her father shrank, disappearing into the sheets and pillows, almost too frail for the double wedding ring quilt with the band of red roses embroidered at the edges.

It was an extravagant quilt with ruby and denim and bright yellow gingham fabrics. Her mother had made the quilt twenty-four years ago after marrying her father. She'd made it by herself and it had taken her an entire year, saving the fabrics, cutting, piecing, and then embroidering. The quilt was her father's favorite thing in the house. He'd never said so in words, but he never let anyone else wash the quilt, or fold it back in summer.

Gently, Ellie smoothed the quilt over his chest, her fingers brushing across the pink and crimson roses near the edge. He closed his eyes, the only sound in the room his ragged breathing.

"Are you comfortable, Papa?" she whispered.

He didn't answer, and she didn't press him, sitting on a chair next to the bed, her hand in his, listening to the air rattle in and out of his lungs.

Footsteps sounded on the wooden floor behind her. "You were up all night with him last night," Thomas said. "Go rest, and I'll wake you in a bit."

She shook her head. "I can't leave him—"

"He's sleeping now. There is nothing you can do. And a couple hours of sleep would help you."

She opened her mouth to protest but just trying to speak made her eyes fill with tears. The fear was suffocating, her exhaustion crippling. She didn't want to break down in front of her father, or her new groom.

"You'll call me," she said.

"Yes."

"And you'll be with him?"

"I'll sit in that chair."

Numbly, she went to her room and struggled out of her wedding dress and put on a nightgown and then her long dressing robe so she'd be ready should Thomas knock on her door before climbing into her childhood bed, in her childhood room.

She didn't feel any different than she had when she woke up, and yet everything had changed.

Shivering, she pulled the covers higher. She didn't want to think, or feel, aware that there was no going back. There would never be going back, only forward.

The emotion she'd kept bottled in all day threatened to spill, but she gripped her covers tighter, and smashed all the emotions down. There would be time to grieve. That wasn't today, or tonight. Her father was still here, alive, and that was all that mattered.

Her eyes closed and somehow, impossibly she slept, only to be awakened four hours later by a firm rap on her door.

"Ellie, you'd best come. He's failing."

ARCHIBALD BURNETT DIED three hours after midnight on Easter Sunday.

Thomas was there, at the back of the master bedroom when Burnett drew his last breath. He knew it before Ellie did, but then he'd gone through this a half dozen times before. And yet once he knew the old man was gone, Thomas felt a lance of pain deep in his chest where his small, hard heart belonged.

Silently, he said a prayer for the old man's soul, and then

he gave Ellie a moment to see if she'd recognize that her father was no longer with her, but when she kept her head down, her cheek still resting on the thin, frail hand, he moved forward.

"Ellie," he said gruffly. "Your father—"

"I know." She lifted her head, her fingers still clasped with her father's.

She was pale, unnaturally pale, her lips pressed tightly. She rose from her chair and gazed down into her father's face for a long minute. Her throat worked. Her jaw tightened. And then she carefully bent close and pressed a kiss to her father's cheek before smoothing his shock of white hair and then doing the same to his bushy beard.

"He went so quickly." Her voice was low and hoarse. "Just days ago he was still himself."

"He hung on for you, despite the pain."

"He never complained about the pain."

"I think if it weren't for you, he would have stopped fighting weeks ago."

She turned to look at him. "You think he was waiting for me to get married?"

"I know he was. Your pa was a good man."

"What happens now?"

"We have the kind of funeral he would have wanted—"

"He didn't want one."

"Then you have the kind of funeral you'd want for him, and then you mourn him and when you're done mourning, you'll get on with living, just as he intended you do."

July 1890

CHAPTER SIX

July 5, 1890

THREE MONTHS AGO today Thomas married Ellie.

Tonight, after midnight, it would be three months since Archibald Burnett passed away. Thomas had kept a calendar and he'd checked off every day since the April fifth wedding.

It had been a long three months for both of them. He'd been working from sun up to sun down on the ranch, aware that he had much to learn and prove, and she'd spent the time mourning. He'd given her the space and time to grieve, too.

And she had grieved. She'd done nothing but grieve since Easter, sequestered in her bedroom, only leaving the privacy of her room when she was certain he wasn't in the house, quickly, quietly entering the kitchen for something to eat or drink before disappearing back into her room where she'd lock the door on the inside. He understood from Mrs. Baxter that Ellie didn't dress. She rarely bathed. She had no needlework in her room, nor anything to occupy herself with. When she emerged for a meal, she didn't sit at the table. She ate alone in her room, and it wasn't just Thomas she avoided, but everyone, Johanna Douglas included.

He'd known she would mourn, and he'd expected her to take to bed for awhile, but as the weeks turned to months, his patience and sympathy wore thin. Unabated grief wasn't healthy. Thomas was concerned she was losing her grasp on reality, the endless mourning making her ill, not just physically, but mentally.

It was time to call her back to the land of the living. Time to give her a sense of purpose again.

She wouldn't like it.

She would fight him. But she couldn't live forever in her bedroom as if a hermit, or a cloistered nun.

PAPA HAD BEEN gone for months, she wasn't sure how many months, but the seasons had changed, the cool spring giving way to bursts of heat in the late morning, a heat that lingered late into the afternoon.

She'd had such good intentions when she'd married Thomas Sheenan. She'd planned on showing him the ranch, and taking him across the vast property personally. She knew the hills and mountain slope that rose up behind the house, and she was going to prove to her husband, that no one knew the property better than her.

But somehow her good intentions failed her after the brief funeral. Once her father was buried next to her mother and the baby girl that had died with her mother, Ellie shattered.

She'd thought she'd been prepared for the loss, but once the casket was lowered, and then the earth began falling on the casket, she sort of lost her mind. She screamed and tried to stop them from shoveling the dirt in. She'd thrown herself at Mr. Harrison as he was the one holding the shovel, and she wouldn't be calmed, forcing Mr. Sheenan to pick her up and carry her still screaming into the house.

She knew at the time her father wouldn't approve.

She knew in the coming weeks that he would have wanted her to get up and get dressed and introduce her husband to the ranch.

But something was broken inside of her. She was broken. She couldn't get dressed. Couldn't speak. Couldn't function.

The weeks turned to months and while April and May were a blur, she'd begun to be aware of the rhythm of each day.

Or at least, the rhythm of her husband's day.

She listened now to his heavy thud of boots on the stairs as he headed down. He'd already been in the kitchen. She'd heard his boots earlier and she'd smelled his coffee on the stove, as well as the bacon frying in the pan.

Every morning he ate the same thing, bacon tucked in to thick slabs of soda bread baked in the heavy skillet, washing it down with black coffee.

She knew because she could smell the rasher frying early

each morning before Mrs. Baxter arrived, and she'd seen the remnants when he'd been called to an emergency during calving and he'd left his breakfast behind, uneaten.

Sitting up in bed, she heard a door close, banging, and then his footsteps on the porch and then all was silent. He was on his way now to the barn. He'd return midday for dinner, and then again at dusk for supper. Even though she managed to avoid him, she knew his routine.

She knew that each night after Mrs. Baxter left, he heated hot water and bathed in the mudroom attached to the kitchen. She knew because she could hear the clank of the copper tub as he placed it on the floor and then emptied it after. She would see his towel drying in front of the kitchen stove each night when she came down for something to eat after he'd gone to bed. He always used the same towel, washing it himself, and then drying it himself. He washed his own linens and work clothes, too. She knew that because Mrs. Baxter had told her during one of their rare, brief conversations.

Mrs. Baxter had been concerned when Mr. Sheenan insisted on doing his own laundry, but when he'd suggested that he'd like to prepare his own dinner and supper, she'd put her foot down. Her job was to clean and cook, and he could take away one of her responsibilities, but not both.

Ellie left bed and pulled on her wrapper, tying it carelessly at her waist before putting her long, tangled hair into an untidy braid. She ought to shampoo her hair but she was so afraid of all the knots that she put off cleaning it, fearing she'd have to cut her hair now instead of just giving it a good wash.

She'd become unkempt and she knew it, but she found it impossible to care. No one saw her. No one wanted her. She just existed now.

Perhaps today instead of carrying her tea back to her room, she'd go sit in her father's chair by the fire in the parlor and put his blanket over her lap. When Thomas was out, she liked to pretend her father hadn't died, that in fact, he was just busy, maybe dressing, or in the barn speaking to ranch foreman, Mr. Harrison, or perhaps he'd traveled to Emigrant to have a drink in the saloon, which would be exciting because then when he returned he'd have news about the neighbors. He'd tell her what was happening in New York, and about the big banks and the stock market.

She loved his news. She loved hearing what he had to say about the weather and the economy and the ranchers that had given up on cattle entirely, selling their land, or defaulting to the banks in Marietta.

Ellie glanced toward the parlor on her way down the stairs. It was dark. No fire burned. Silly Papa. Why had he let the fire burn out?

Ellie would build the fire and then she'd prepare a lunch for her father and Johanna and her to enjoy. Johanna hadn't come calling in weeks. Maybe she'd appear today and amuse them with stories of demanding ladies needing gowns urgently, despite Marietta being in the middle of nowhere.

Papa always enjoyed Johanna's visits. He said it was likely she'd end up a spinster, but Johanna didn't seem to mind being single as she had her own business and it gave her an excellent income. Johanna was lucky to be successful and independent. Truly, she had the best of both worlds.

As Ellie headed for the kitchen, Mrs. Baxter passed, head down, eyes downcast, too. Ellie felt a pang because once upon a time she and Mrs. Baxter had been relatively friendly, but Ellie couldn't bring herself to speak, not to anyone. Not even to Johanna, which was why imaginary conversations were so much more satisfying. It allowed her to remain in seclusion without feeling overwhelmingly lonely. Johanna would be appalled, though, at Ellie's fantasy life. But Johanna didn't know, and even though her friend had stopped by numerous times right after her father's funeral, even dragging a chair into the hall and waiting for Ellie there, but despite a ten-hour vigil, Ellie wouldn't unlock the door, or see her, or speak, and Johanna finally left, and hadn't returned since.

Ellie was thinking about Johanna's last visit when she entered the kitchen and it took her a second to realize she wasn't alone. The kitchen wasn't empty.

Ellie froze halfway across the floor, heart tumbling, gaze fixed on the massive man seated at the kitchen table.

Thomas Sheenan.

It was as if she'd never seen him before and everything in her screamed outrage that he was here, in her home, invading the sanctity of her space.

It had been ages since she'd seen him, the night of her father's funeral, as a matter of fact. She wasn't sure how long ago that was, only that the chill of early spring had given way to the heat of summer. She'd gone from sleeping with quilts piled on her bed to wanting just a sheet most nights.

Confronted by his very real, very physical presence, she didn't know where to look, or what to do. He sat, facing the doorway, in the oldest and largest chair at the table, long legs extended, tall leather boots crossed at the ankle, the dark brown leather scuffed.

The man was huge, seeming to fill the entire kitchen, and worse, he looked so comfortable, sprawling in the chair, *her father's chair*, thick black hair tousled, long, powerful limbs relaxed. He looked at her openly, intently, as if he owned the chair, the table, the kitchen itself. Indeed, he looked quite at home.

Impotent rage filled her. Her hands balled at her sides in her skirts. She felt like a child's bouncing ball caught in the middle of a hard bounce. She practically twitched with energy, her emotions as violent as the intensity trapped inside of her.

She'd never liked him, and right now she thought she could hate him. Acid burned her throat. Her stomach churned.

"That is my father's chair," she said roughly, her voice hoarse in her own ears.

It had been weeks since she'd last spoken. Or perhaps it'd been longer. And the effort to speak cost her. She felt almost dizzy with the effort.

The big Irishman shrugged, unmoved. "All the chairs look the same."

"That is not true. That chair is the largest. It has arms on it. I am sure you knew that—"

"Perhaps I did, perhaps I didn't."

"Move."

His broad shoulders shifted carelessly. "I'm sure your father wouldn't mind—"

"But I do." Her gaze met his. "There are three other chairs at that table, please take another."

"No."

She blinked, astonished. Had he actually just refused her? And refused her so impolitely? She exhaled sharply, the air hissing from between clenched teeth. Why had she married him? Why hadn't she chosen Mr. Baker? Mr. Baker would never have spoken to her so crudely. Mr. Baker would have treated her with kindness and respect. "I beg your pardon—"

"I accept your apology. Nothing else needs to be said."

Her heart did a hard, livid thump. Her pulse raced far too fast. "I wasn't apologizing. That, *sir*, is my father's chair. It is off limits, just as his chair in the parlor is off limits, his room, his books, and anything else that was his."

Silence descended and Thomas didn't appear inclined to break it. Instead he looked at her from beneath his lashes,

lashes that were far too black and thick, his hard, chiseled features without expression.

The silence continued to swell and grow. Ellie felt the weight of the silence as if it'd wrapped around her, suffocating her.

Her throat swelled closed. Her eyes burned. "Are we clear?" she added shortly, barely able to breathe. It felt as if she'd just run a very hard, fast race and it was impossible to get enough air.

"We are clear on a few things. Shall I remind you of them?" he drawled. When she didn't answer, he ticked off on his fingers, "One, your father is gone. He's not coming back. Two—"

"Do not speak of him!"

"If you wish."

"I wish."

He leaned forward and pulled out the chair next to him at the table. "Two, we are married, and you are my wife, so please, have a seat. It's been a long time since we've spoken."

"I'm not staying down here."

"You need to eat."

"I can eat later."

The corner of his mouth lifted but the smile didn't reach his eyes. "I'm not going to work outside today."

"It's not even the Sabbath. How lazy. My father—"

"Is dead." He drew the chair back even farther, the wooden legs scraping the worn planks of the kitchen floor.

"*Sit*, Mrs. Sheenan."

Sit, as if she were a dog or an unruly child.

Sit, as if she was his to command.

Sit, as if he expected her to obey.

Heat surged through her, the blood rushing from her middle, up, across her chest, and higher to her neck to scald her cheeks. "Whom do you think you're speaking to?"

"*My wife.*" He rose, and tapped the back of the chair. "So have a seat, Mrs. Sheenan, or I'll put you there myself."

He was imposing sprawled in the chair, but overwhelming standing, looming over her the very way Copper Mountains shadowed Marietta. She took a panicked step backward. "Have a care, sir. Keep your distance. I'd hate to have to shoot you, but I would, in self-defense."

"I doubt your gun is on your person at this very moment."

"I'll go get it."

"And then shoot me in cold blood?"

"If I had to."

"Wouldn't you find that difficult to explain to the sheriff? You ran upstairs and retrieved your gun to shoot your husband because he asked you to sit with him for breakfast?"

"If my husband threatened to touch me, yes."

"By putting my hands on your waist, over your dressing gown?" Thomas arched a black brow. "Shocking."

"I'm glad to be a source of amusement for you, but let's be very clear on one thing. I have not given you permission to touch my person. And I will not give you permission. We had an agreement—"

"You don't even honor your agreements, so don't make too much of them." He pushed the chair toward her. "Now sit and I'll put the kettle on. Let's try to put the histrionics aside, at least while we have a cup of tea."

She edged back toward the doorway even as she kept a close eye on him. "I'm going to my room. I'll have Mrs. Baxter bring me a light luncheon later."

He watched her take small steps, one, two three before announcing, "Mrs. Baxter has been relieved of her duties here at the house."

The news blindsided her. "*What?*"

He shrugged as he dropped back into her father's chair. "There isn't enough for her to do to justify the wages—"

"Of course there is—"

"I do my own laundry, I prepare my own supper. What you eat every evening in your room, is the meal I have prepared while you hide away upstairs in your bed. It's wasteful to pay someone for work that doesn't need to be done."

Her head was spinning. She didn't know how to process everything he was telling her. He hadn't just been doing the cooking in the evening, he'd been quite good at it, but that wasn't the point, though, was it? He wasn't supposed to be cooking. He wasn't supposed to be interfering in domestic matters. The house was her concern, not his. "You had no right to make that decision. You do not pay her wages and what she does, or doesn't do, is none of your business."

"You forget, Mrs. Sheenan, that this is our house, and our ranch—"

"It's my father's!" she screamed, close to losing all control. "This is the Burnett Ranch."

"But there is no Burnett working this ranch. There is no Burnett anywhere that I can see. As such, it's the Sheenan Ranch, and it has been the Sheenan Ranch for nearly three months now."

Ellie's legs wobbled. She exhaled with a painful whoosh. "You changed the deed?"

"At the courthouse, yes. As well as the sign at the entrance of the property. This is now our ranch, in our name—"

"I am not a Sheenan, I am a Burnett, and this is the Burnett Ranch."

"It was, yes, until you married me, and you were a Burnett until you married me, and now you are a Sheenan. You are Mrs. Thomas Sheenan."

Her eyes closed and she held her breath, holding in the wild emotions that threatened to break free. She couldn't keep shouting, and she certainly wouldn't let herself cry in front of him, but how dare he? How *could* he? "You have deliberately destroyed my father's legacy," she said, eyes opening, blinking hard to hide the sheen of tears. "You did it out of spite."

He hooked one arm over the back of the chair. "You are

your father's legacy, and the children we have will be his legacy."

"We're not having children. I'm not having anything to do with you! I want you out. I want you to go right now."

"Alas, love, it doesn't work that way. This is my house now. My property. My livestock. My livelihood. I'm not leaving, not ever."

"Then I'll go."

"Will you now? And where will you go, and with what money? As your husband, I control the purse strings."

"So I have nothing?"

"I'll give you an allowance, but you'll have to do your part. You won't get something for nothing."

"And what is my part?"

"Your wifely duties."

She blanched. "In your bed?"

"Later, yes. But for now, cooking. Cleaning. Tending to our home."

"That is Mrs. Baxter's job."

"But Mrs. Baxter is gone—"

"She's not gone. She's upstairs."

"She was upstairs, yes, but she slipped out the front door five, maybe ten, minutes ago. I saw her leave."

"She didn't say goodbye. She didn't tell me she'd been fired."

"Why should she? When was the last time you spoke to her? When was the last time you spoke to anyone who worked here, never mind lived here?"

He sounded so calm, so arrogant, and smug. And it was his smugness that made her stomach rise and her chest compress. He had no idea that anger made her stronger, or that he'd picked the wrong adversary. She was no meek, biddable woman. Her father had raised her to have a backbone, and she might have lost her father, but she still had a spine. "How clever you are. How proud you must be."

"I wouldn't say clever, or proud, no. Determined would be more accurate."

Fury and frustration washed through her. She couldn't stay, couldn't listen to another word. Heartsick, Ellie left the room, chest on fire. She was so angry she shook from head to toe as she climbed the stairs to her room, her legs weak, her right hand trembling on the banister. This couldn't be happening. He couldn't mean half the things he said, and he certainly couldn't mean that he'd actually, legally changed the name of the ranch. That was the worst. *That* would be the lowest of low.

Eyes stinging, she closed the door of her room and turned the key in the lock, then leaned against the door, hands fisted, knuckles pressed to the wood.

If he truly changed the name of the ranch, she hated him, and she would hate him forever.

CHAPTER SEVEN

A ND THAT WAS just round one, Thomas thought, leaning back so that his chair rested on two legs as Ellie's bedroom door slammed shut above.

He'd expected the fire and fury. He hadn't minced words or tried to protect her from the changes on the ranch. She needed to know. She needed something to care about, something to fight for, and she'd fight for the ranch. She'd fight for control. He welcomed the battle. It had been far too quiet in this house for the past three months. He was a loner so he wouldn't have minded the quiet if he lived alone, but every day he'd been aware of Ellie upstairs, locked in her room, locked in with her grief.

Grief was part of life. Death was a given. No one would escape it. But, eventually, one had to commit to living, and they did that by function and making decisions and taking action. Thomas was determined to see Ellie outside again, this week. He wanted her riding and being part of the ranch management. He wanted to see her dressed and heading into town.

In short, he wanted her to be the woman he married, not

this wraith slipping in and out of rooms when she thought the house was empty.

With a sigh, he put the chair down and washed his hands and face at the sink before slicking his hair back with damp hands before exiting through the back door.

It was only mid-morning but outside temperatures were rising. It would be another warm day but for now, the air still smelled sweet, and fresh, scented with baked earth and summer hay.

Birds warbled in the tall tree adjacent to the house.

Thomas headed for the barn, willing himself not to think of anything now but the work ahead of him. Nothing would be gained at this point by worrying about Ellie, or dwelling on the hard things she said. He'd expected a fight, and she'd given him one. Good for her. He would have been disappointed if she'd meekly caved in and sipped her tea and promised to behave as if a proper wife. He certainly didn't have feelings for her as a wife. He didn't know what he felt for her, only that he knew he was responsible for her, and he'd promised her father he'd look after her, so he'd do that. Thomas didn't make many vows, but when he did, he kept them.

Will Harrison, the ranch manager, nodded as Thomas entered the barn. Thomas gave a barely perceptible nod in response and continued to the horse stalls, stopping at Archibald's big palomino and giving him an affectionate pat. He greeted each of the horses until he came to Oisin's stall.

The tall black stallion stared at him, ears and nose twitching and Thomas leaned on the gate.

"Soon," he said gruffly, watching the unhappy horse. "She'll be back. It won't be long, I promise you."

Oisin took two steps toward Thomas, stopping just out of reach.

Smiling faintly, Thomas reached into his pocket and pulled out the core of his tart apple from his lunch earlier. Palm flat he offered the core to the stallion.

Oisin gave him an indignant look, but after a moment, he took the core in his teeth, lips peeling back to avoid contact with Thomas's skin before backing up.

Thomas's amused smile faded after a moment and he shook his head. "You two deserve each other," he said, before continuing through the barn to the pen outside where the cowhands were in the process of weaning the bigger heifers they intended to take to market in the fall from their mothers.

It had been a busy three months since he'd moved into the Burnett Ranch house. He'd arrived in the middle of calving season, and they'd only just finished calving when lambing began. Four years ago, Burnett Ranch had started with three hundred sheep, and now had nineteen hundred ewes. Thomas thought two thousand would be a comfortable number, but Harrison was pushing for almost twice as much. Privately, Thomas wasn't sure that the land could sustain both cattle and sheep if herds were that big, but so far

Thomas had kept his opinions to himself. Things were less awkward now than when he arrived early April, but he still felt like the outsider. Thomas knew farming in Ireland, but it was different in Montana. Everything was different in Montana—the harsh weather, the vast size of the properties, the rugged terrain. And so even as Thomas threw himself into the work, he was aware that the others were watching, not just Harrison, but the other hands, and they all watched him, waiting for the misstep, waiting for him to fail. But he wasn't going to fail, and he did what he always did—he worked longer and harder than the others. He started earlier, worked later, and worked smarter, too. It might take a full year for Harrison and the hands to fully accept him, but they would, eventually, and if they didn't, or couldn't, then by next April, those hands would be replaced. It was hard enough trying to step into the shoes of the legendary Archibald Burnett, much less run one of the biggest spreads in Gallatin, Crawford, and Park counties, without having any employees on his side.

IT STAYED LIGHT late during Montana summers and since Ellie hadn't wound her clock since her father died, she had to use her senses to tell her what time it was. And it had to be past six in the evening by the rich, savory aroma wafting upstairs, creeping under her door, making her mouth water and her stomach growl.

She hadn't had much appetite these past few months. She'd only nibbled at food and from the loose fit of her dressing gown, she'd lost weight. She didn't care about the weight. In fact, she didn't care about anything. That was the problem and she didn't know how to begin caring again.

She'd known she'd miss her father but she hadn't expected this... despair, and she missed little things she hadn't anticipated. The bracing scent of her father's shaving soap. The rich tobacco smell of his pipe. The quick smile he'd give her when she entered the room. His habit of tugging on his moustache, keeping the points sharp. And then the sweet way he'd call her Ellie girl.

A lump filled her throat. She missed everything about him, but most of all she missed his love. And now her father was gone and a stranger lived in the house. There was nothing familiar or comforting about Thomas Sheenan, either.

She perched on the side of her bed, her stomach rumbling, hearing the clank and bang in the kitchen.

She was hungry, and irritated, and in a terrible mood. She'd been in a foul temper ever since this morning when Thomas told her he'd changed the name on the title of the deed. That he'd turned the Burnett Ranch into the Sheenan Ranch.

It made her want to throw up.

He couldn't have been more disrespectful, or hurtful, if he'd tried. But even then, she wasn't going to let him chase her out of her own kitchen. This was her house, not his, and she refused to hide upstairs just because he was downstairs.

He was the outsider, not she.

He was the one, making things unpleasant.

She needed to regain control. She needed to put him in his place. He'd all these weeks to grow comfortable in the house, but it was time he remembered that she was in charge here, not he. She was the mistress of the house, and would always be mistress of this house, and no Irishman, no matter how big or how intimidating, was going to make decisions for her.

Simmering, she took off her dressing gown, changing into her blue gingham before heading downstairs to see what was happening in *her* kitchen. She found him at the stove, his beige linen shirt clinging to his shoulders, outlining the width of his back as he used a wooden spoon to stir something in the big black cast iron skillet.

"Supper is almost ready," he said, still facing the wall, somehow aware that she'd entered the room although she hadn't made a sound. "Please lay the table."

How had he heard her? It was as if the man had ears in the back of his head. "I'm not eating with you," she said quietly, stiffly. "I'd like a word with you and then I'll be taking my meal to my room."

He glanced over his shoulder at her, expression impossible to read. "We can discuss whatever you like over supper—"

"Thank you, but no. I prefer my own company."

His eyes met hers, the dark irises glinting with something she couldn't understand. For a long moment he said nothing, his gaze just holding hers, and then his lips thinned. "In that case, you'll be preparing your own supper."

"Fine."

"So what is it you wanted to discuss?" he asked, dishing a generous plate of roast beef.

The meat was so tender it fell apart as the thick slices hit his plate, splashing juice onto the mound of mashed potatoes.

Her stomach growled. She didn't think she'd ever smelled anything quite so appetizing before. She forced her attention from the plate to his profile. "The paperwork for the ranch. I'd like to see it."

"Why?"

"I just want to see if you actually changed the name."

"I actually changed the name." He turned around. "Are you sure you don't wish to join me? You haven't eaten all day."

"I found some bread and cheese, so I'm not starving." It wasn't true, but he didn't need to know that. She did know that if she joined him for a meal, he'd view it as a victory and she'd rather starve than give him the satisfaction of thinking he'd beat her.

Because he hadn't beaten her. He hadn't won.

"You're being stubborn," he answered, holding his plate out to her. "You can fight with me tomorrow, but tonight, eat. It'll do you a world of good."

It probably would, too, she thought, as emotion bottled in her chest, closing her throat, making her eyes burn. She was tired and hungry and sad and she hated him for taking her home—her father's home—and turning it into his place.

She hadn't cared that his name was Sheenan until now. His name hadn't been an issue… until he'd used it to erase her father.

"Take it," he said, more forcefully, a lock of black hair falling low on his brow, shading his dark eyes.

Black stubble covered his jaw and his white shirt fell open, exposing not just his throat, but part of his chest. She looked away from the blatant display of skin and muscle. It was indecent. He was indecent. An Irish never-do-well.

"You had no right to change the name of this property. It's been Archibald Burnett's since he carved it from the valley thirty plus years ago. He put up the fences and he plowed the field and planted crops where there were only rocks."

"Your father knew it would happen after he was gone."

"But I didn't!" Her voice rose, pain sharpening her tone. "I'm shocked, and angry, and it horrifies me that you'd do such a thing when my back was turned. How can I trust you? How can I respect you, never mind like you?"

"All good questions," he answered. "And I'll try to answer them if you'll sit down with me and have a meal with me—"

"No. Never. I'd rather starve."

"As you wish, m'lady." He gave her a slight bow before carrying the cast iron skillet to the slop pail in the corner and dumping the remaining roast and gravy into the pail.

Her jaw dropped as he returned to the stove, and plopped the skillet down, making the skillet rattle.

He'd thrown away the supper. All of it. What a waste. And then shock turned to outrage as he pulled out her father's chair and sat in her father's place. "Must you sit there?" she choked, voice strangled.

"You're not staying, so what does it matter to you?"

"Because it's where my father sat my entire life."

"But this is also where I've sat every morning and every evening for the past three months." He lifted his head, his dark gaze skewering her. "Until this morning, I didn't know it was your father's chair. But I do know why he sat here. He could see the door from this seat. He could also see out the window. It's a defensive position allowing him to react quickly should he need to. It's why I will continue to sit here."

"Even if it upsets me?"

He looked at her so long that her skin prickled uncomfortably.

"You want to be upset," he said eventually. "You are looking for a reason to be angry with me."

Her heart hammered and her pulse jumped wildly in her veins. She was so angry she couldn't even think straight.

"Rest assured, you've given me more than sufficient ammunition."

SHE WAS IN the middle of a dream, a warm lovely dream, and in the dream she was happy, and there was sunshine and lots of warmth and laughter, the kind of warmth and laughter at Christmas or some other special time, and it was beyond irritating to be pulled from such a lovely dream by the sound of banging.

And the banging came from below.

Bam, bam, bam.

Sleepily, Ellie rolled onto her back and listened. It was very loud, and very even. Bam. And again. And then again.

She sat up and pushed her coverlet aside. What was Thomas doing? Was something broken?

What was he hammering? And why was it so loud? She glanced at her window and it was only just dawn, pale pink fingers of light streaking the horizon. And why so early in the morning?

Uneasy, Ellie left her bed, opened her door, and moved to the top of the stairs. The noise had stopped but now there was a muffled sound coming from the kitchen. Footsteps echoed from the kitchen and then finally silence.

She came down the stairs, and as she reached the bottom step, she looked toward the kitchen doorway, or where the doorway had been, because the door was gone, covered by thick roughly planed lumber.

It took her a second to realize that the kitchen had been boarded up. That Thomas Sheenan had boarded the kitchen.

Was he insane?

The front door opened and the man in question walked in. He saw her, she knew he saw her, but he ignored her as he passed her in the hall, continuing on to the stairs where he took them two at a time as if intending to go to his room, the small guest room tucked under the eaves at the very back of the second floor.

"What did you do?" she said to his back, voice shaking with outrage.

He paused near the top to turn. The hall was nearly dark, no lights on but she didn't need a lamp to hear his sarcasm. "You weren't interested in cooking, so I've closed the kitchen."

"And how do you intend to prepare your meals, Mr. Sheenan, when the kitchen has been barricaded?"

"I'll use the kitchen door. I have a key to the deadbolt."

"And me? What about me? Am I to starve to death?"

"I hope not."

"You're mad," she choked.

"Maybe."

"You admit it?"

"I admit that I'm tired of doing all the work. I'm also tired of fighting you."

"You wouldn't have to fight me if you just left me

alone!"

"As I did for the past three months?" He laughed roughly, no humor in the deep sound. "That was a mistake. Just look at you. When was the last time you combed your hair or put on a clean dress? You smell—"

"I don't!" she cried, outraged.

"Your skin is greasy. Your hair—"

"Enough. Leave me be." Her voice broke. "*Please.*"

"I can't. I won't. Not any longer."

"Why? What I do shouldn't matter to you. Nor should you care how I look, so if you don't like my appearance, don't look at me! You didn't marry me for love, or affection. You married me for the land. And you have the land. You have what you wanted. Count your blessings—"

"But I don't have you."

She stiffened. "What does that mean?"

"This isn't a marriage. I want a marriage. We agreed to a marriage."

"We agreed we'd wait."

"To consummate the marriage until we became acquainted, but how are we to become acquainted if we don't take meals together, or speak to one another? I don't think it's asking too much for you to sit at a table with me, or to prepare toast and coffee for me."

"I'm not ready to become acquainted—"

"When will you be ready?"

"I don't know." She stared up at him, outwardly defiant

and yet on the inside, she was reeling. She wasn't ready for this. She wasn't ready for him. "You need to give me time."

"It's summer, Ellie. It's been three months since your father's funeral."

"Do not use my name!"

"You're my wife."

"No."

"*Yes.*"

She looked away, mutinous, emotions rioting. She'd made a terrible choice marrying him. There was a half dozen Marietta and Bozeman, decent, respectful bachelors who would have made a better match. Why hadn't she picked one of those men? "You do not get to dictate how much time I'm allowed to grieve. It is my grief, not yours, and my life, not yours—"

"You are my responsibility, and as such, I am insisting you to return to the land of the living. I appreciate that you lost your father. But you can't just remain in bed. There is work to be done. You are needed to contribute to your family's welfare."

"What family? You?"

"It's a shock, isn't it, Mrs. Sheenan?"

She hated him using her first name, and yet she hated being called Mrs. Sheenan even more. Good God but this was a nightmare. She wasn't at all prepared for life with him. "And what do you expect me to do, Mr. Sheenan?"

"What other wives are doing right now. Putting away

food for winter. Planting late summer crops—"

She laughed out loud, cutting him short. "I do not pre-serve food. I don't make applesauce or jam or pickles. I do not butcher or dry meat. If you feel the need to begin preparing for winter, then please, chop all the firewood you want, and once you have sufficient firewood, head into the mountains and look for grouse and deer and elk but, Mr. Sheenan, for me summer is about picnics and parties and enjoying the fine weather, not laboring next to a hot stove."

"Is that what you've been waiting for? A picnic? In that case, bathe and I'll take you on one. This afternoon."

"I don't want to go on a picnic with you. I don't want to do anything with you. I want my father back and my old life back—" She broke off, voice strangled, dangerously close to breaking down. She clenched her hands, digging her nails into her fists.

Dear God, she needed to pull herself together. She couldn't fall apart here, now, in front of him. She couldn't weep as if a child. Her father didn't tolerate tears. If she was going to cry, she'd do it in the dark, in the privacy of her own room. Ellie drew a deep breath, and then another, concentrating on slowing her breathing and regaining control. "You say I am mistress of this house. Do you mean that?"

"Of course."

"Then take down this barricade so I can access my kitch-en, or neither of us will ever get anything to eat."

"You have access to the kitchen through the mudroom door. All you have to do is go outside and walk around to the back. It will be good for you. Fresh air. Exercise. A chance to view your property from someplace other than your bedroom window." He paused, his face shadowed in the dim light of the stairwell. "You might not appreciate my tactics, but I am trying to help you."

She made a soft sound of disbelief in the back of her throat. "Do not take me for a fool, Mr. Sheenan."

"I do not, Mrs. Sheenan." He started to move away then stopped. "I will leave the kitchen door unbolted so you have access to the kitchen and laundry during the day. The back door is unlocked now, and I would very much enjoy a light meal, toast and cheese, or a scrambled egg would do. I don't want to overwhelm you. Let us start with something simple to avoid taxing you."

"I don't feel like cooking."

"Then slice the bread and serve it with butter and cheese. I'm going to change my shirt and I'll be back down soon."

And then he continued down the hall toward his room, leaving Ellie bristling at his authoritative tone. Who did he think he was, ordering her about? And did he really think he'd get anywhere with her, acting as if he was the boss, and she was in his employ?

Jaw gritted, she turned to look at the boards nailed to the doorway trim, the rough planks hiding the entrance.

It was crazy to block off the kitchen. She'd married a lunatic. She was just glad her father wasn't alive to see this.

FIFTEEN MINUTES LATER, Thomas entered the kitchen, pleased to see Ellie there. She was sitting at the table, finishing a slice of bread with a thick curl of butter.

He glanced around the kitchen, checking the stove and counters and tabletop to see if she'd prepared him anything. She had not.

He pointedly looked at her.

She lifted a brow. "You didn't actually expect me to make you anything when you treat me like a servant in my own home?"

"You're not a servant in this house. You are the mistress of this house. And as mistress of this house, one would think you'd want to take care of those residing under your roof. For most women, it is a point of pride, but they are excellent hostesses."

Ellie's lips compressed and her gaze clashed with his. He could feel her anger, her fury and resentment palpable in such a small space.

He held her gaze, undeterred by her tight, defiant expression. If she wanted a battle of wills, she could have it.

He would win, though, in the end. He always won.

He was tough, hardened. A survivor. Consumption took five of his family members, but not him. He, his mother, and middle sister, Eliza, had nursed the others through the disease, before his mother contracted it, and then finally Eliza. They all died, every one of the five, but him. There was no reason for him to escape unscathed, but he had.

It was almost a curse, surviving.

Small, stubborn Ellie Burnett Sheenan had no idea what she was up against, and he stood there, in front of the stove, and stared back at her until she finally averted her head, her cheeks flushed red.

She rose stiffly and crossed to the cupboard to retrieve a plate. At the table, she cut a thick slice of brown bread, and then spread butter on it and shoved the plate across the oilcloth, toward an empty chair that wasn't hers, or her father's. "There. You're welcome."

"Thank you," he said, approaching the table and taking the plate from the spot she'd put it and carrying it to the seat he'd chosen as his own.

But before he could sit down, she swiftly yanked her father's chair away from the table, pushing it behind her to keep him from sitting in it. They were standing close, just inches apart. He could easily reach out and touch her, or take the chair back.

"You will not win," he said softly, meeting her defiant gaze.

She didn't shrink from him. If anything, her green eyes blazed, fire in the depths. "You don't frighten me. You are just a big bully."

"And what am I hoping to achieve by bullying you, my

sweet bride?"

ELLIE HEARD HOW his voice dropped, and deepened. The husky note made her nerves tighten and tingle, her lower back suddenly exquisitely sensitive and the hair on her arms and at her nape rising. She drew a quick painful breath. "You're trying to force me to bend to your will."

"It would be nice if you stopped fighting me."

He was so tall that he towered over her, dwarfing her, and then Ellie reminded herself that her father had been tall, too, and she'd grown up around strong men. She wasn't going to be intimidated. She lifted her chin and looked up into his eyes. "It would be nice if you could find somewhere to go that wasn't in my house."

His lips quirked as his dark gaze bored into her, letting her feel his tension and impatience. His muscular body hummed with energy. It was a palpable thing, nearly as palpable as the intensity in his gaze. "I will work Monday through Saturday on the property. On those days I'll leave early and return late. But Sundays we will spend together. Today will be spent together." And then he sat down in her father's chair.

Ellie counted to five, and then ten, and finally fifteen.

She couldn't let him upset her like this. She couldn't give him so much power over her. She'd gone to bed livid and angry, but she didn't want to start a new day angry.

Instead she went to the wooden cupboard and took out the canister of coffee beans and poured beans into the small metal grinder. He'd made coffee earlier but she wasn't about to drink his.

He noted what she was doing. "There is still coffee left in the pot on the stove."

"Yes, but it's your coffee and I know you don't like sharing," she answered as sweetly as she could.

"I have no problem sharing."

"Really? Then why did you throw away the roast last night?" She let her eyebrows rise, her expression innocent. "Or perhaps I misunderstood you?"

"You didn't misunderstand."

"You like being wasteful."

"No."

"Or maybe you are so rich that it doesn't bother you to throw away perfectly good food."

"Apparently, I am a wealthy man, and I had no idea how wealthy until I went to the Bank of Marietta and met with Henry Bramble. He was happy to go over the accounts with me."

Her insides churned. He hadn't wasted time getting to know his net worth, had he? "Is there anything you don't know yet?"

"You. You're my big mystery."

She didn't even try to answer that. Teeth gritted, she twisted the grinder handle, crushing the beans, wishing she could crush him as easily. She despised him. Everything about him. He wasn't at all the man she'd thought she'd married. Baker, Fridley... any one of them would have been a more suitable groom than this Irishman.

"I know your father used to take you to town on Sundays so you could see friends, so I've invited your friends over for an early supper," he said when she'd finished grinding. "Mr. and Mrs. Douglas accepted, and Mr. Douglas's sister, Miss Douglas—"

She froze. "You what?"

"I invited them to supper."

"Here? Tonight?"

"They're worried about you, and I know your father would not want you taking to your bed for months on end. He'd want you up, riding, and socializing—"

"You don't know him. You have no idea what he'd want."

"I know your father never spent weeks in bed, not even with his cancer. It was only his last day that he took to bed, and he wouldn't approve of you locking yourself in your room now. Harrison told me your father believed in fresh air and exercise, but you're not getting either."

"Mr. Harrison talks too much."

"Mrs. Baxter agreed with Harrison. She said he must be rolling in his grave—"

"I'm glad Mrs. Baxter is gone then," she interrupted fiercely. "I thought I could trust her, but I see I was wrong."

Thomas's mouth firmed. "Harrison and Mrs. Baxter are trying to help you, and your friends, the Douglasses want to help you."

"Thank you, but I don't need help from any of you."

"But you do. You can't keep going on as you have, and so, while I gave you those three months—three uninterrupted months—to mourn, it's time to return to the land of the living and take care of your responsibilities."

"My responsibilities?"

"Your house and your husband."

Ellie's stomach fell even as her face went hot then cold. She prayed she'd misunderstood him. "*Excuse me?*"

"Yes, you lost your father in April, but you also became a bride. I've been here three months without so much as a word from you, nor have you walked your property, visited your horse, or taken care of our home. You are the mistress of this house, and entertaining friends tonight will give you a chance to catch up on news and enjoy yourself in your own home."

"I am not ready to entertain."

"Left to your own devices, I'm not sure you ever would be, which is why I'm helping you by inviting people over who love you, and miss you—"

"Send word that supper is cancelled."

"I'm not going to do that."

"Do I look ready to entertain? Do I seem like I'm ready to cook for a large group?"

"I'm happy to help you with the meal, if you like."

She laughed, feeling almost hysterical. Had he lost his mind? "No. And no. And no again! I don't know who you are, or what you think you're doing, but I am not going to take orders from you, and I have no desire to see anyone, not even if they are my closest friends. I'm sad, Mr. Sheenan. I'm angry and upset and"—she broke off and drew a tremulous breath—"devastated. I'm *devastated*. And I'm not going to entertain just because you're tired of me spending my days alone in my room. It's my room. And I want to be alone."

"And you are my wife. My bride. And I am ready for my wife to act like my wife, not like a crazed woman whispering about the house late at night and early in the morning. From now on you will rise when I rise, and prepare me breakfast before I leave for the day to work and on weekends, we'll entertain, or go to town and have a meal there. But we're going to live, and we're going to do it together."

"Are you well? I'm worried you might be feverish and confused, because I am not your servant, or employee. I have never made anyone's breakfast except on Sunday when Mrs. Baxter didn't work and even then I would prepare a light meal for my father. So, on Sunday, whenever that is, I'll make you toast and tea at a decent hour, not early, but an hour that is suitable and convenient for me."

"Today happens to be Sunday, Sunday July sixth, and we'll skip the tea and toast today to give you more time to prepare supper for our guests."

"You must have either a hearing loss, or a mental deficiency, because I've been quite clear that I'm not ready to entertain. Send one of the hands to let the Douglasses know that supper has been cancelled."

"All the ranch hands have today off. It's Sunday. A rest day. And we're not going to cancel now, not when the invitation was extended five days ago."

Her jaw dropped. "It baffles me, sir, that you'd extend an invitation without consulting me."

"I'd hoped company would cheer you."

"I don't want to be cheered. I don't want to be pleasant and gracious—"

"I'm well aware of that."

"If there is no one available to ride to the Douglasses and cancel the invitation, then you must do it."

"I'm not cancelling."

"I'm not entertaining."

"Then saddle your horse and go tell them yourself."

She gestured to her rough, matted hair. "You know I can't go out like this!"

"Then do something about it."

"I think that's enough."

"I'll stop when you take action. You need to remember who you are." He gestured to her hair and then robe. "This isn't who you are. It's time to pull yourself together."

Ellie's heart was racing so fast she could barely breathe. He was so unbelievably callous. She'd never met a man so hurtful. "You're not helping."

"Do you want me to bathe you? If so, I can. I'll bring the tub in, and heat the water—"

She picked up the coffee grinder and flung it at him. It just missed his head before crashing to the floor, spilling beans and grounds everywhere. "Get out!"

He rose from the table and stepped over the mess. "An excellent suggestion."

THOMAS CLOSED THE mudroom door behind him.

Round two had proven to be even more volatile than round one, which wasn't a total shock considering he was the one who'd boarded up the kitchen, and then casually announced that they had three guests coming for dinner.

Even though they didn't.

They would, soon, but it wasn't happening today. She didn't need to know that now, though. What she needed to do was return to the world of the living, and if it required a shock to the system, so be it.

He'd meant to get her attention this morning, and he had. Were the tactics kind? No. But eventually she might thank him.

Maybe not until she realized that Sinclair Douglas and his wife and sister weren't coming to eat this evening, but hopefully by then, she'd at least be clean, and in a pretty dress, and trying to pull something together for a meal.

Thomas didn't want a banquet. He wasn't anticipating anything fancy or formal. He just wanted to see some effort on her part. He wanted to see her *doing* something.

In the barn, Thomas saddled his horse, eager to go for a good, long ride while it was still cool. He glanced at Oisin as he led his horse, Crockett, from the stall. Crockett had been Archibald's horse, the big handsome red stallion named after Colonel David Crockett who died in the Alamo.

Thomas wanted to get Ellie back on her horse, riding, soon. His goal was to have her riding by next weekend. He hoped he wouldn't have to tie her to her saddle to make it happen.

As he thought of her, he remembered how she'd chucked the coffee grinder at him, and how it just missed his head.

She was a hellcat. And trouble. But the fact that she was up, and trying to make coffee this morning was progress, and progress was what mattered most to him.

When he'd first met her, she'd been beautiful and elegant, a fiercely proud woman with a fiercely independent mind and tongue. But now she reminded him of a stray in dire need of a hot bath, a decent meal, and some obedience training. He could handle the training. Hopefully she'd take at least care of the bath.

AFTER THOMAS LEFT, Ellie finished making coffee and ate some breakfast and then confronted the big copper tub in the mudroom.

She didn't know where Thomas went, or when he'd come back, but now seemed to be the right time to bathe and try to deal with her hair. Just thinking of her hair made her touch the thick braid. It was rough and coarse and tangled beyond belief. She'd tried to work the tangles out on several occasions but gave up when she kept breaking the teeth in her favorite comb.

Dragging the tub into the kitchen, she placed it close to the stove and began heating water. She didn't need to fill the tub all the way, but she did want the water to be slightly warm.

Holding her breath, Ellie removed the ribbon from her braid and began to loosen her hair. This was not going to be easy, or painless.

THOMAS RODE FOR an hour and then returned to the barn where he rubbed down his horse and then cleaned the bridle well.

He tried to stay busy, not ready to go back to the house, but he felt a niggle of worry as he used the leather soap on the straps and took apart the bridle, cleaning each of the metal bits one by one. As he worked, he kept an ear toward the house, wishing he wasn't uneasy, and not even sure why he was worried. He'd left her many times before. He'd gone to town before and hadn't thought twice. So what was bothering him now?

Growling with frustration, Thomas threw down the rag he'd been using and left the barn, his strides long, worry making him hurry. Reaching the back door, he opened it and was about to enter the mudroom when he saw that the copper tub was gone. She must have moved it for a bath. He hesitated, listening. At first he heard nothing, and then there was a soft sniffle.

And then another.

He frowned, thinking it sounded suspiciously like crying. Suppressing a sigh he called to her, "Ellie, are you all right?"

She didn't answer him.

He pushed the door wider. "Answer me, Ellie Sheenan, or I'm coming in."

"Don't!"

"Then tell me what's wrong."

"It doesn't matter. Just stay away."

"Are you in the bath?"

"Yes."

"Did you just get in?"

"No. I've been here forever."

"Then get out. The water must be cold."

"It is."

"Wrap up in a towel and I'll remove the tub. You must be shriveled like a prune by now."

"I can't," she said faintly, her voice cracking.

"Why not?"

For a long moment she didn't answer, and then she said, her voice whisper soft, "Because I need help."

Something in her voice made his chest tighten. She sounded scared, and teary, and far too vulnerable. "Are you hurt?" he asked gruffly.

"No. But I've made a mess of things and it's just getting worse."

"What can I do?"

She hesitated then choked, "I need you to cut my hair for me."

"*What?*"

"Don't sound like that. I'm already really upset. Just get the scissors from my father's desk—and if you can't find those, then maybe the shears from the barn—because I need you to cut my hairbrush out. It's too knotted and there is no way to get it out now—" Her voice broke and she made a soft hiccupping sound. "Please just do it quickly and promise you won't look at me."

"I'm coming in."

"Not without the scissors!"

He ignored the command, and pushed the door open, entering the kitchen. The kitchen was on the east side of the house, which meant it was bright in the morning but dim late in the day. But even in the shadows, he could see Ellie's pale back and slender shoulders and the thick red hair that looked like a bird's nest billowing around her head.

She grabbed for a towel sitting on the stool, sending water splashing. "You're looking!"

"You're my wife."

"We had a deal."

"There is far too much negotiation in this relationship. So be quiet and let me see what you've done."

Her eyes were enormous as he approached her, her lips quivering. "Just cut it out," she said thickly. "Just do it fast and be done with it."

"Stop telling me what to do, woman. It's annoying." He crouched next to her, and tipped her head down to have a look at the back of her head where he could see just a bit of the wooden handle of the brush, the stiff boar's bristles entirely hidden by the angry tangle of hair. "How did you do this?"

"My hair was knotted and I couldn't wash it properly, and I thought maybe brushing it would help get some of the knots out. Instead it just knotted it even more."

"I knew I should have stayed—"

"It wouldn't have made a difference. I wouldn't have let you help me." Her pale slim shoulders rose and fell, her hunched spine revealing every knobby vertebra. She reached up with a trembling hand to swipe beneath her eyes. "And I still don't want your help but it seems I have no choice."

She might be thin, and trembling, but there was still fight in her voice. He was glad she couldn't see his smile. "Why don't you want my help?"

"Because you'd say something rude about my hair being

filthy and that's why it's such a mess and I'm tired of feeling bad. I don't like feeling this way." She pressed the towel tighter to her chest. "So will you please just cut the brush out and let me finish washing my hair so I can get out of this tub and begin making a meal for people I don't want to see?"

"Why don't you want to see them? They are your friends."

"Johanna is, but the others aren't. Her brother dumped me—" She broke off, lips compressing. "It doesn't matter. I just can't believe people are coming and I've ruined my hair, and I liked my hair. I loved my hair and now it will be chopped short and I'll look like a boy, and not just a boy, but an orphan boy, and I don't know what we'll eat—" She broke off again as he laughed.

Her head tipped back and she looked up at him, outraged. "Why are you laughing?"

There were men who would probably think her most beautiful when dressed in one of her fine gowns with the jaunty bonnets that showed off her bone structure to perfection, but he didn't think she'd ever been so appealing as she was now, with her bare skin and soft, pink mouth, and her green cat eyes shimmering with tears. Angry tears.

"Because even orphans need love," he answered gravely, praying his lips didn't twitch.

Her eyes grew brighter, fiercer. She clutched her towel tighter. "Do not mock me!"

"I can't help it. You are so fierce and prickly. You remind

me of a cat in the bath."

"I beg your pardon!"

Thomas reached for the stool, dragged it toward the tub and sat down, the tub between his thighs. "Let's get this brush out of your hair, shall we?"

"Just cut it. We don't have time for this."

"We have time," he answered.

"It's too tangled, I promise you."

"Do you want me to cut your hair off?" he asked, aware of her gaze sweeping him, and lingering for a moment on his thighs before she blushed and looked away.

"*No!* But at the same time, I don't want guests arriving and finding me still in the bath with a rat's nest on top of my head."

He smiled inwardly. Hellcat. "What if I told you that no guests were arriving?"

She froze. "Is that true? Did you cancel the invitation after all?"

"Mmm," he answered noncommittally. "Now sit still, be patient, and let me see what I can do about this brush you've attached to your hair."

He was the one, in the end, who proved his patience. Untangling the brush took at least a half hour of painstaking work, unraveling the bristles hair by hair, lifting the brush a smidge up, and then down, and once he finally had the brush free, he took a comb to the rest, working at each knot, even the hopelessly thick ones that had proven impossible for her to remove earlier when she'd first tried to shampoo and detangle her hair.

"You never invited them," Ellie said suddenly, breaking the silence. "You didn't cancel the invitation. You simply never invited them in the first place."

She couldn't see his face but she could have sworn he was smiling.

"Why do you say that?" he asked.

"Because you wouldn't board up the kitchen before people were coming. You wouldn't want them to see that."

"Oh, I wouldn't say that. I don't care what people think. Never have."

"Yes, but I just don't think you'd do that now. I think you were trying to scare me. Rouse me to action. Am I right?"

"Did it work?"

She exhaled in a rush. "Thank goodness. I've been panicking about what to make for supper and if I could get away with serving sliced ham and bread and summer fruit."

"I don't see why you couldn't. I'd be happy with such a meal. It sounds perfect after a hot summer day."

"It is hot outside, isn't it?"

"It's warm here on the valley floor, but if you ride up in the hills it's nice."

"Is that where you went today?"

"Yes."

"I miss riding."

"Join me next time."

"Do you ride well?"

"You probably ride better."

"And shoot better," she added smartly.

"I don't know about that, but I'm sure you're a better shot than my sisters were. They never even handled a gun before, much less had one of their own."

"You had sisters?"

"Yes. Four."

"And brothers?"

"Four."

"There were nine of you?"

"Yes. I was the fifth," he answered working at yet another impossible knot. "I remember how our mam would introduce us. She'd always go in order. Joseph, James, Mary, Martin, Thomas, Eliza, Catherine, Patrick, and Biddy." He paused as he took the edge of the comb to the knot, trying to ease the tangled strands of hair. "I never knew Martin, he died when I was just a baby."

She stayed quiet as Thomas kept talking. She sensed he was trying to distract her from the tedious task as he told her how his oldest brother, Joseph, had left home at sixteen, going to London to apprentice himself in trade.

In the beginning, Joseph sent money home regularly. Not a lot, but he always made a point of sending something, but then he was arrested for stealing, and found guilty, and before he knew it he was on a ship to Australia, and they never heard from him after that.

She twisted around to look at Thomas then. "What happened to him?"

Thomas shook his head. "We don't know."

"What did he steal?"

"Meat or pies, I was never sure which."

Ellie frowned. "That's terrible."

He shrugged. "James, the second oldest, had always been very tight with Joe, and so despite my mam's objections, he indentured himself so he could go to Australia to look for our Joe."

"Did he ever find him?"

"No. But James landed on his feet once there. He worked for a farmer on a big sheep station. Lots of red dirt and sun but James took to it okay and when he was done working off his fare, he kept on working for the McCully's, and he saved his money so that he could bring me out and maybe one day we'd have our own farm together."

"So why didn't you go out there?"

"Because he married a woman who didn't like the Irish."

"Have you stayed in touch with him?"

"It's been a while."

"How long is a while?"

"Five years, maybe more."

She was silent a moment, digesting this. "So you came to America because of an uncle?"

He took the comb and used a tooth to pick at one of the

worst knots just below her nape. He didn't say anything for awhile. "Not because of him," he said at length, "but because of what he said about Montana. About the mountains and the sky and how there were valleys so pretty it hurt your eyes."

She felt her lips curve. "Your uncle sounds like a poet."

"Give an Irishman enough drink and he'll become a poet."

"So you left the rest behind… what's the name of your town?"

"Rathkeale, it's in County Limerick, not far from Kerry. Kerry is pretty. Rathkeale not so much. It's home to tinkers—"

"Tinkers?"

"Gypsies."

"That sounds romantic."

"It's not. Trust me. They have a different code of conduct than you or I. You can't bargain with them, or trade with them, because they won't honor it. The only people they are loyal to are their own."

"And you left your mother and sisters behind with them?"

"I didn't leave them—" He broke off, set the comb down and rose. "It's getting dark in here. I can barely see what I'm doing. Let me light a lantern."

When he returned, he set the lantern on a chair next to them, the soft yellow light creating a warm golden glow.

"My oldest sister, Mary, married and moved to Dublin. The rest of us—me, Eliza, Catherine, Patrick and Bridget, who we called Biddy—were still at home. I was the oldest of those still at home, and I worked on a big estate near our house. I didn't earn a lot, but my wages were necessary and made sure we at least had something to eat. We'd grown up without much, and our neighbors didn't have much, and that was just the way it was."

"So you were happy?"

"Happy enough," he answered, hands gentle as he worked at yet another knot, careful not to pull at her hair or scalp. "I don't think we really thought about it. And then Mary came home from Dublin sick. Her husband sent her and the baby back to us, thinking that rest and fresh air would help her cough. Eliza and Mam took care of Mary while I went to work each day, and then when I came home, I'd take over in the evening so they could rest."

Ellie pressed her chest to her knees, sensing that the story was about to take a dark turn. She hoped she was wrong.

"Five weeks after Mary returned home, Catherine started to cough, and then almost immediately Patrick and Biddy. Mary and her baby died first. A month later we lost seven-year-old Biddy. Biddy was the family darling. And they just kept dying... Catherine. Patrick. Mam." He swallowed hard. "Eliza was the last."

For a moment there was just silence, a heavy aching silence that made her realize how much he missed his family, and how much he still grieved for them. But she didn't know how to comfort him, or if he even wanted her to comfort him, and before she could think of something vaguely appropriate to say, he'd risen from the stool and crossed the room, leaving her.

Shivering, Ellie hugged her knees, watching him walk to the cupboard. He stood there for awhile, not doing anything, and she chewed the inside of her lip, feeling the hurt that hung in the room. He was trying to gather himself. And just when she was about to thank him for his help, and let him know she could manage the rest on her own, he was reaching into the cupboard for a bowl, and then a glass bottle and then an egg from the small wooden crate on the counter.

He cracked the egg into the bowl and took a fork to it, whisking it. "This was my mam's recipe for the girls' hair. My sisters had the thickest, shiniest hair in our town." His voice rasped, his accent strong, making the words sound lilting.

He'd loved them so much.

Her eyes burned and her chest squeezed, smashing the air in her lungs. And still she couldn't think of the right thing to say. Maybe it's because there was nothing right that one could say. Sympathy didn't bring back the dead, or ease the loss.

In the glow of the lantern, he looked big and alone, and yet for the first time it struck her that he hadn't been raised to be a solitary man. He'd been part of a large, tight-knit family.

She watched as Thomas poured a generous measure of the bottle into the bowl, and immediately recognized the smell as castor oil. He began whisking again as he walked toward her. "You're not going to make me drink that, are you?"

The corner of his mouth slowly lifted. "No."

"Thank goodness. I'd have to fight you."

"As if you don't already."

She adjusted the towel, making sure it was firmly sandwiched between her chest and her bent knees. "You've seen nothing yet."

"Oh, I don't doubt that." He sat down on the stool again, the tub between his long legs, his powerful thighs on either side of her. "But the good news is that the brush is out. Most of the tangles are out. There are still lots of small matted pieces, but this will help. I'll rub it in and leave it on for quarter of an hour and then begin combing it through. It should help detangle the rest, and it'll condition your hair, too."

"Cutting the brush out would have been faster."

"That was never an option. I love your hair. It's too beautiful to chop off."

She was filled with warmth, and she blushed at the compliment. "I bet you didn't know you'd be spending hours messing with my hair today."

He lifted the rough weight of her hair, and poured some

of the egg and oil into it, massaging it in. "I knew you were going to wash it today. I just didn't know I would be involved."

"How did you know I would be washing it?"

"It was on my to-do list."

His confidence astounded her. Ellie tipped her head back to give him a setdown, but when she looked up, he was smiling and he arched a black brow, making him a little too handsome and rakish.

"Tis true," he said, giving her head a nudge, so he could pour more of the mixture onto the top of her head, before quickly working that in as well.

No one had washed her hair since she was a little girl, and it was altogether too intimate having his strong fingers massage her hairline and scalp. It wouldn't bother her as much, though, if it didn't feel so good. He seemed to find each of the pressure points on her head, and he'd knead at them, easing tension and sending rivulets of pleasure through her.

She'd never felt anything half so good in all her life. The man had wickedly talented hands. Clearly, he'd done this before and she felt a stab of jealousy that other women had enjoyed his ministrations.

For long minutes, he continued to massage the egg and oil into her hair, focusing first on her temple, and then above her ears, below her ears, along her nape and then slowly worked his way up the back of her skull to the top, making her melt. Perhaps her new husband wasn't completely useless…

"What did you say?" he asked, his deep voice close to her ear.

She stiffened and looked up. "I didn't say anything."

"You did. It was something along the lines of not being completely useless."

Had she really spoken her thought aloud? Mortified, Ellie flushed, heat washing through her, from her belly up to her breasts, neck, and cheeks. "I was referring to the castor oil," she said quickly. "That it's not completely useless."

He said nothing.

"I would have never thought of it as a hair tonic," she added, wishing she'd just stop talking.

"Hmm," he answered, his tone suggesting he thought the same thing, too.

Ellie wanted to shrink into the tub and disappear.

"Lean forward," he said, scooping up her long hair to better work the oil and egg into the ends before reaching for the comb with the widest teeth.

THOMAS HEARD HER soft sigh of pleasure as he slowly drew the comb through her hair. He worked her hair in sections, first the ends, then the middle, and then finally from the top to the bottom, stopping when he hit a knot and then he'd carefully remove the knot, and try again.

"Are you sure you weren't married before?" Ellie asked him in a soft voice.

Thomas smiled faintly. His wild cat was practically purring. "Not married, but I had those four sisters. Usually they'd wash each other's hair, but after they were sick, I'd do what I could to make them comfortable."

And suddenly, just like that, his throat had closed, and his chest was hard, and tight, and it hurt to breathe.

From the moment he'd uncapped the castor oil, he'd thought of them all, the smell taking him immediately back to Rathkeale. His mother used to threaten the younger ones with it when they wouldn't eat, or if they misbehaved. He'd only had to drink it once, and the intense laxative property had cured him permanently from giving his mam sass.

The only one who'd never had to take it was Biddy. Biddy was the family baby, and the most affectionate of them all.

Biddy's death had broken his heart. She adored him, and he her. But Eliza... Eliza wasn't just a sister; she was his friend and confidant. She knew him better than any, and she'd nursed the others tirelessly. When she became ill, Thomas made deal after deal with God—spare her, and Thomas would go to Australia. Or spare her, and Thomas would take her to America with him. Spare her, and he'd marry a local girl and set up house and Eliza would live with them...

But she wasn't spared and when her coughs produced

blood, she apologized to him for making him worry. She was sorry to be a problem, and even sorrier that he'd have to manage things on his own.

If he closed his eyes, he could still see her. She looked the most like him, but instead of brown eyes, hers were blue. She was always smiling, always in good spirits. Like Biddy, Eliza was quick to laugh, quick to encourage, easy to hug.

He missed his sisters. And little Patrick, so serious, so determined to be a man. Patrick, with his old soul, was going to be a priest, and do good, and heal the sick, and feed the poor.

His eyes stung, and his stomach cramped and for a moment he couldn't do anything but close his eyes and will the pain away.

The memories were too much. It was easier not thinking of them, easier not remembering, and yet at the same time, if he didn't remember them, then it was as though they'd never existed and that wasn't fair… not to them, and who they were, and how important they'd been to him.

"Did you have a favorite sister?" Ellie asked in a small voice.

"I was very close with Eliza."

"She was the one who died last, wasn't she?"

He winced. "But I doted on Biddy," he said, his deep voice harsh to his own ears. "We all did. She had the sweetest, kindest disposition. A little angel, my mam called her."

Ellie said nothing more.

"I'm going to get a bucket of fresh water to rinse your hair." He rose and walked out.

ELLIE WATCHED HIM leave, a lump in her throat, realizing she could no longer dismiss him as a cold, hard man. That wasn't a fair or true assessment, as Thomas had layers to him, layers and layers, and beneath all, just maybe a heart, as well as the patience of a saint. She wouldn't have been able to do what he'd done this afternoon—detangling her hair for hours, and never once criticizing her for allowing it to happen in the first place. She owed him her gratitude, and probably a light supper.

Thank goodness he said he didn't mind ham and cheese and summer fruit.

CHAPTER EIGHT

T HOMAS COULDN'T SLEEP and he punched his pillow, twice, and when that didn't help, he flipped it over and tossed back the covers trying to get cool.

But even then he couldn't get comfortable.

It was late, well past midnight, and yet he couldn't unwind, continuing to question everything that had happened this afternoon, and regretting the decisions he'd made.

Discovering Ellie crying in the bathtub had rattled him. He could handle her anger, he understood that she was stubborn, but when she quietly wept, he couldn't walk away from her. Nor would he cut her hair. Under no circumstances would he cut her hair.

He'd taken the stool and tackled the task of working on the knots and tangles, never letting her know just how difficult it was unraveling the brush, strand by strand, when she was practically sitting in his lap. Having her naked and so close had tested his control.

Even with the knots and tangles, and eyes pink from crying, she was beautiful, her skin pale and smooth, her mouth full and soft.

He'd tried to distract himself by focusing on the tangles, and yet beneath the thick clumps of hair he could see the length of her back, her spine supple and strong, her porcelain skin flawless. He'd felt a jolt in him when his fingers brushed her warm shoulder. She felt as soft as she looked and when she sat up a little, stretching, arching, he'd hardened, and for the next hour he just ached, unable to ease the heavy erection he was trying desperately hard to hide.

He told her about his family not because he liked sharing, but because he needed to do something to take his mind off her naked body and the fullness of her breasts peeking from the side of her hand towel.

He shouldn't want her like this.

He shouldn't want to strip the towel away and reach for the sponge and wash her all over, beginning with her breasts and ending with the hidden "v" between her legs.

Groaning with frustration, and the heavy ache of yet another erection, Thomas climbed from bed.

His small window was already open and he leaned on the high sill, breathing in the fresh night air. He had to cool down. He had to calm down. He'd never sleep if he remained half erect all night.

And he really wished he'd kept his stories of Rathkeale to himself.

She didn't need to know about his family. He'd never told anyone about his past, or how his family had died, and he regretted sharing with her. His past was personal and painful, and better left buried, like his four sisters, and Margaret's baby, and Patrick, and Mam.

Forehead pressed to the glass, he stared out at the night with its half-moon. And even though he was seeing the moon over Montana, he was remembering how the moon looked from their flat in Rathkeale. They didn't own their flat on the third floor, and there were more of them in their two bedroom flat than the owner liked, so they were always trying to be quiet, and keep from disturbing their neighbors, although the neighbors complained anyway. Hard not to complain when the family above you was dying, one by one.

There were only two bedrooms on their floor. The girls had one, the boys another, and at first their mother slept in a corner of the main room, but after his two oldest two brothers left, Mam moved into the room with Patrick and him. They hung a curtain down the middle to give her some privacy, but there was little privacy for a big family in a small flat, and there was almost no way to escape disease when they lived so closely together.

In all fairness, Mam and Eliza had tried to keep everything clean. They kept the house spotless, in fact. But the illness spread anyway.

Thinking of them made him feel slightly mad. Why had they been cursed? And why had he escaped? It wasn't fair. If they were going to die, shouldn't he have died, too?

Thomas arrived in America angry. He'd worked in New York for six months to save up money to move west, and then he was in Chicago for a year, before going to Nebraska, South Dakota, North Dakota before finally going in search of that uncle in Montana. His uncle was gone but Thomas liked Montana, and he'd found work in Bozeman before moving east over the hills to Livingston and then down to Marietta.

By the time he found a job in Marietta, he'd been in America for six years and no longer was he the brash, hot-headed Irishman looking for a fight, but a man ready to own a piece of the American dream, which for him was hard work and sacrifice.

The American dream wasn't a wealthy wife.

The American dream didn't include a wife at all.

Thomas drew a slow breath, trying to slow his thudding heart. He shouldn't have stirred the memories. He was better with the door firmly closed on the past, better without emotions, and desire, and yet tonight he was full of both. Grief for his lost sisters, and an aching desire for a wife that shouldn't be his.

He'd done nothing to earn Ellie, and he'd done nothing to deserve her, either.

This afternoon when he'd rubbed the egg and oil into her hair, massaging her scalp, she'd leaned back against the tub, head tilted, eyes closed with pleasure, dense lashes fanning her cheekbones.

She'd sighed softly as he worked the paste, and sighed again as he found sensitive spots on her skull—the temple, the crown, just above her nape. His thumbs massaged each of the sensitive spots, soothing nerves and easing tension.

It was the first time in this new marriage when he thought that it could maybe work, and that maybe they could be happy. Or learn to be happy. At least, in that moment, he was happier than he'd been since marrying her, because for once he wasn't the man he despised, the rough, uneducated Irish immigrant who'd made an excellent marriage simply by being in the right place, at the right time.

No, yesterday he'd felt like a man with a beautiful young bride, and he delighted in her beauty, focusing on her soft sighs of pleasure, and how with each exhale, she relaxed a little more, shoulders dropping, elegant neck exposed, firm chin up, her full lips ripe, and so very appealing.

If they weren't still strangers, he would have taken her mouth, kissing it until she opened for him, giving him access to the inside of her mouth, and then eventually her body—

Thomas stopped himself there.

He'd never be able to sleep if he kept thinking about her, or thinking of how she must look now, in her bed, long red hair spilling across her pillow, slender curves covered by a crisp cotton sheet.

No, he wouldn't ever sleep if he thought of her. It had been months since he'd been with a woman, since before Christmas actually. The last time he'd been with a woman was the night before the big mine explosion and fire.

The night before he first met Ellie. After glimpsing Ellie

from the fire wagon, he'd lost all desire for other women.

He didn't even know who she was that night, only that she was the most vivid, vibrant woman he'd ever seen and, when her bright gaze met his, he wanted her like he'd never wanted anyone. But what could he offer a woman like her? Sex? Companionship? How would that ever be enough when breathtaking Ellie Burnett wanted the world, with all its pleasures, including forever love?

SOMETHING HAD CHANGED during the night. Ellie could feel it the moment she entered the kitchen the next morning and spotted Thomas at the table, in his favorite spot.

He seemed different, and she didn't know why, and wondered if it was really him that was different, or if she was possibly viewing him in a new light.

But no, it was him, she realized, as he glanced up, looking at her in a way he hadn't yesterday, or the day before.

This morning he looked at her as if she was a woman, a woman he found attractive, and the frank curiosity and interest sent a shiver racing through her.

"Good morning," she said breathlessly, grateful he didn't know her thoughts otherwise he'd know she'd had the most restless night, her sleep punctuated by dreams of him, dreams that were uncomfortably sensual.

"How did you sleep?" he asked.

She blushed, remembering her dreams. "Well," she lied.

"And you?"

"Good."

And then she glanced away because she was suddenly nervous and shy and she wondered if she'd even thanked him the night before for helping her. She wasn't sure because last night had ended in a strange rush of good nights. He'd seemed anxious to leave her, and she'd felt confused by the abruptness of the goodbye. "If I didn't thank you properly last night—"

"You did," he said.

"I am grateful."

"No more thanks are needed."

"Yes, but it took hours."

"If you're uncomfortable with the time I spent detangling, stop. I did it for myself. I like your hair long and didn't want to see it chopped off just to free a brush."

She couldn't help reaching up to touch her hair, the heavy mass twisted and pinned into a simple but elegant chignon. It was a relatively uncomplicated style, but not easy to execute with her hair so clean as the silken strands kept tumbling out, requiring twice as many pins as usual. "Did your sisters have long hair?"

He shifted in his chair. "Yes, but I'd rather we didn't discuss them anymore." His voice was pitched deep. "If you don't mind."

"You don't like speaking of them?"

"No."

"Why?"

His broad shoulder shifted. "I'm not good with the past. I don't like the memories."

"But surely there must be good memories as well—"

"I should get to work," he said abruptly, rising and pushing back from the table.

She'd just crossed to the stove to check the coffeepot and paused to glance out the window over the sink. The sky was still pitch dark. There wasn't even a hint of light on the horizon. "What time is it?"

"I imagine it's close to five."

"Why begin working now? It's still very early."

"I always do. I like to get a head start on my day."

She filled the empty cup waiting for her on the counter and then carried the cup to the table. "But not even Mr. Harrison, or the hands, begin work until after seven," she said sitting down.

"Exactly. This way I am always the first one there. I like to settle in before the others arrive."

"And Mr. Harrison never said anything to you?" she asked, wishing he'd sit down again. He was far too tall when standing.

Thomas's shoulders shifted. "Why should he say anything? It's not his ranch."

"But he's worked here for over twenty years," she said, brow creasing, uneasy with his tone. It was almost as if he wanted to pick a fight with her now. What had she said that upset him? "I just thought that maybe you would have consulted him—"

"And I have, if I've a legitimate question, but when I work, and what time I show up, doesn't require his input. I appreciate his loyalty to your father, but he works for me, not I for him."

She nearly dropped her cup. "Have you said that to him?"

"It's not necessary to spell it out. He knows, and I know."

It was on the tip of her tongue to comment that he'd made himself quite comfortable, but she didn't want to say that, knowing it would result in a fight, and they were finally getting along better so the last thing she wanted was to quarrel with him.

And yet, he was still new here, and he'd never managed a cattle ranch of this size before.

"You disapprove," Thomas said.

She hesitated. "I'm just... surprised."

"Why?"

"I don't know."

"Not true, you do."

She drew a breath, wishing they hadn't started on this topic because it wasn't going to end well. He wouldn't like that she had opinions, and more so, that her opinions didn't align with his. "I just hadn't thought it necessary to change the way things are done here, and I'm sensing that you've made some changes on the ranch."

"If I've made changes, they were for the better."

"But when you're still so new here, how do you know the changes are for the better? Wouldn't it have been wise to settle in and observe how Mr. Harrison manages first, or maybe consult me, and ask what I think?"

"You haven't been available, Mrs. Sheenan," he said curtly, downing the rest of his coffee and carrying his cup to the sink.

From the back he looked immense, his shoulders broad, his spine rigid. He was angry.

"Although I suppose after the wedding I could have taken to my bed, too," he added. "Maybe that would have suited you better."

She said nothing, her jaw clenched, as annoyed with him as she was with herself. She'd known she shouldn't be honest with him. Her father might have welcomed her opinions but Thomas Sheenan didn't.

Her silence seemed to gall him because he turned around, his arms crossed over the thick planes of his chest, fabric taut over his bunched biceps. "Would you have been happier with a wastrel for a husband? Would that please you, my lady?"

"You're trying to pick a fight with me," she protested, "and I don't want to quarrel—"

"No, you just like making little jabs, humiliating jabs to keep me in my place."

"That's not true."

"It is true and, to be fair, I'm the first to recognize that I do not belong here. Every day here I'm conscious that I'm an outsider, and only in your house because you ran out of time and couldn't find a more suitable husband."

"That can't be a comfortable thought," she said after several moments of silence.

"No, it's not."

"But you know I've thanked you. The day we married I expressed my gratitude."

"And I suppose I'm to be grateful for that?"

She frowned, her patience wearing thing. "What do you want from me?"

"Something else than this," he muttered, grabbing a biscuit from the sideboard and then the thick slices of bacon and heading for the mudroom.

She rose, trembling with anger. "And to think I almost started to like you."

He turned in the doorway. "Oh, don't do that, Ellie Sheenan, because then we might actually have a real relationship, one requiring respect and give and take—"

"But that's what I want!"

"No, you don't. You want to be the mistress, in control, with me as your boy trotting at your heels."

Her hands balled at her sides. "You didn't have to marry me! Nobody put a gun to your head so don't blame me if you're unhappy."

"I'm not unhappy with the ranch. I have no problems with Harrison."

"I see. Your issue is with me."

"I appreciate you've been busy these past few months staring at the ceiling, but while you've locked yourself in your room, I've been working my ass—"

"There is no need to swear!"

"Trying to succeed here, and I don't need you criticizing my decisions when I'm giving everything I have to make this work."

She couldn't take a breath without feeling the horrendous lump in her throat. He was so rude, so completely despicable. "Take your bacon and biscuit and go. Your chores are calling you!"

His lips curved and his dark eyes narrowed, a dangerous gleam in the brown depths. "Oh, I think my morning chores are right here."

He hadn't moved and yet she suddenly felt the need to back up, but when she took a step, her hip banged the edge of the table, and her knee collided with the chair. There was nowhere to go, not without a dramatic shove of her chair, and the last thing she wanted to do was let him know she was uncomfortable. Animals could sense fear. And right now, Thomas Sheenan reminded her of an unpredictable animal.

"I'm sorry if you found my words offensive," she said quietly, proud of her calm voice, as well as the fact that she was the one trying to make amends.

But he wasn't soothed. "How could I not find them offensive?"

"I'm trying to make things better," she snapped.

"How?"

"I never called you a wastrel, or useless. Those were your words, not mine."

"No, you didn't. That was true. But it wouldn't cross your mind to thank me for taking on the responsibilities of the ranch, or to feel gratitude that for the past three months I've woken before dawn to be sure I'm the first one in the barn, that it's deliberate I'm there before the others so they can see by my actions that I'm not just here to freeload, but I'm committed to the property, and most of all, you."

She felt his tension from across the room. "Of course I'm grateful."

"But *of course* you don't sound it. It would kill you to show me courtesy." He moved from the sink and stalked toward her, his dark gaze fixed on her face, his long steps deliberate.

The room seemed to shrink as he advanced. The air bottled in her lungs. She squeezed her hands, palms damp. "Are you trying to frighten me?"

"Are you frightened?"

"No." But she took a step back, bumping the table again.

He didn't stop until he was directly in front of her, so close that she had to tip her head back to meet his gaze, and then when she did, she wished she hadn't. His expression wasn't friendly. There was nothing conciliatory in his eyes or the set of his hard jaw.

She dropped her gaze to his chin, still every bit as rugged as the rest of him, but it was safer somehow, less intense than his burning eyes and grimly twisted lips. "I don't know why you're quarreling with me," she choked.

"Funny enough, I believe that."

She risked a glance up, and then wished she hadn't. His dark eyes smoldered with heat, and something else, something disconcertingly fierce and primal, as if one of those huge Yellowstone wolves was patrolling the valley.

But Thomas wasn't a wolf, and she wasn't part of his pack. There was no reason to fear him. And just because he had a predatory gleam in his eye, didn't mean he actually wanted her. He wasn't hungry. He wouldn't hurt her. If anything, he was testing her, trying to intimidate her, but she wouldn't be cowed.

"I think you've made your point," she said lowly, fingers flexing to ease some of her nervous energy.

"And what point would I be trying to make, *Mrs.* Sheenan?"

She averted her head, hating to be called that, especially in such a mocking tone. "You know this is hard for me. I don't know why you must make it more difficult."

"I admired your father. There was a great deal to like. But as a parent, he failed you—"

"Do not speak ill of him." Her shoulders squared and her

cheeks flamed. "He was a wonderful father, in every way."

"Because he let you have your way, on everything. You're spoiled, selfish—"

She lifted her hand and slapped him across the face, the crack of her palm against his cheek horrifyingly loud in the kitchen.

Ellie exhaled hard, frightened. Even without looking at him, she knew she shouldn't have done that.

Apologize, apologize. Her heart beat frantically as he leaned even closer, the shape of her fingers distinctive on his cheek. She stared at the red handprint in shock.

What was wrong with her?

Why did he bring out the worst in her?

"I'm sorry," she said quickly. "That wasn't right, and my father would not condone me striking you. He would be appalled, so please don't blame him. Blame me. I have a temper, and he did try to curb it, he did. I won't even give you the excuse of saying I'm a redhead because that's not it. It's just me."

And then tears filled her eyes, tears she hated because tears were a weakness and she wasn't going to be weak in front of him. "I'll work on my temper, I will, but please don't criticize him. I miss him so much and it hurts me that he's not here."

"You're the strangest kitten," he said under his breath. "Just when I want to shake you…"

She looked up into his eyes and they were dark and full

of things she didn't understand. "Did you call me a *cat*?"

"A kitten."

"Which is a cat."

"So yes, I did."

"Well then, Mr. Sheenan, you're a wolf."

Grooves formed at his mouth, amusement flickering in his eyes, easing the darkness she'd seen there moments ago.

"I wouldn't argue with that," he answered, reaching out to follow one of the coiled curls she'd pinned up. He tugged on the curl, loosening it, pulling it free of the pins.

"Don't," she said, trying to save her hair but it was already too late. Glossy strands of hair were tumbling free, spilling over her shoulder.

He ran his fingers down, over the curl, as if savoring the feel. "Do you know anything about wolves?"

"I was raised with them—" She looked up into his eyes. "Not in the house, of course, but you can hear them at night, and then when you're riding in the back country."

"We didn't have wolves in Ireland, and so when I first moved here, I met a science professor who taught at Harvard, and he came to Yellowstone to study the hot springs, but after several encounters with the wolves in the park, he decided he wanted to study them. And do you know what he found? That the wolves kept the same mate, and that the leader of each pack, which is called the alpha—"

"I know what alpha means."

His voice dropped and deepened as he leaned even closer. "The alpha male only wants the alpha female, and they only breed together."

She was afraid to breathe because he was so near now his chest was almost touching her breasts. She could smell the soap he'd used for shaving this morning. He also smelled of smoke and coffee.

Heart galloping, she looked from his chest, to his strong chin, and then up to his mouth, fascinated by the shape, his lips neither thick nor thin, but just right, and she swallowed hard, unable to look higher, and yet unable to look away.

She wanted him to kiss her, and just the thought made her skin prickle, lower back tingling, nerves sensitive all over.

And then it didn't matter that she hadn't made eye contact.

It didn't matter that she was trying so very hard not to breathe and not to move, desperate to keep that last remaining inch of space between them, because his hands settled on her upper arms, and he slid them up to her shoulders, and then across her collarbone where his thumbs lightly stroked her delicate skin.

"We agreed," she said hoarsely, voice strangled, adrenaline escalating the intensity of her emotions.

"Agreed to get acquainted," he retorted, his dark head dropping, blocking the light, and she knew right before his mouth captured hers that he was going to kiss her and, in that moment, she stiffened, lips parting to protest.

His lips covered hers then, claiming her mouth as if she

were his, and had always belonged to him. She'd been kissed before. Sinclair had kissed her the night she'd accepted his proposal, and then again the night of their engagement party. In both instances the kisses had been nice—quite pleasant, actually—and she'd looked forward to more once they married, but this kiss was nothing like Sinclair's.

The kiss was neither safe, nor polite. No, this was a kiss of possession. Of a man confident that he had the right to kiss his wife.

Her hands went to his chest to push him back but he ignored the half-hearted attempt, one hand circling her nape and the other low on her back, urging her closer.

He was hard everywhere and impossibly warm. She shivered at the sensation of him against her, and he stroked up her back and then down again. It felt so good to be touched, and yet there was a danger in the delicious caress.

She pulled back, breathing heard, head spinning. "Just how acquainted do you intend us to be?"

His dark eyes glowed. His lips curved. "Very, very acquainted, my sweet."

"You are not abiding by our agreement."

"I never actually agreed to anything."

"You did!"

"No, I just listened to you talk about the agreement."

She pushed hard at his chest. "Release me!"

"Why? I'm not hurting you."

"You're making me very uncomfortable."

"Am I?"

She gave him another ineffectual shove. "Yes!"

"Hmmm. Maybe I need to make you more comfortable." And then his head dropped, and his lips took hers again, the kiss softer, lighter, his mouth brushing the corner of her lips, and then the bow of her upper lip, the kiss so teasing that she couldn't help the shivers racing up and down her back.

"Not helping," she said hoarsely.

"Good to know," he murmured, his lips settling on hers in a long, warm, slow kiss that made her feel as if she was melting. "Better?" he asked, lifting his head an inch.

"No."

"Hmmm. Strange." And then he licked the seam of her lips and she gasped.

The parting of her lips gave him access to her mouth, and his tongue traced her upper lip, and then just inside the tender lip, finding nerve endings she didn't even know existed. Ellie shuddered and he held her closer, shaping her, molding her to his enormous frame—thighs, hips, chest. His strength was dazzling, nearly as intoxicating as the heat rising inside of her, a warmth that made her brain feel mushy and her senses drugged.

He was too good at this, she thought woozily, and the longer he kissed her, the more she welcomed the heat and the pressure of his muscular chest against her breasts and the strength of his thighs. He was hard where she was soft and his strength was far too seductive. Being in his arms made her want to yield to him, and give herself over to him—

But what would happen then?

Ellie stilled, panic flooding her. Her hands were still against his chest and she gave him a short, hard shove. "I think that's more than enough, unless you intend to take more without my consent?"

Thomas released her slowly, but he didn't move away. She smoothed her skirts, creating a sliver of space between them.

He gazed down at her, one eyebrow lifting. "Happy?"

Not entirely. She'd been so warm in his arms and now she felt chilled. "Yes, thank you."

"My pleasure," he answered, a hint of mockery in his deep voice.

She looked up at him, searching his dark eyes and hard features. "You can't be mad at me. I did not initiate the kiss."

"Correct. I did."

"And you did it knowing how I felt about…" Her voice faded as she searched for the right word. "Intimacies."

"You're shy because you're inexperienced—"

"That's not true. I've been kissed before."

"Have you?"

"Yes. And I'm quite… comfortable… kissing."

"Huh."

He didn't believe her. She saw it in his expression and heard it in his voice. She flushed hotly. "Sinclair kissed me.

And for your information, he kissed nothing like you."

"How disappointing." His gaze met hers and held. "For you, I mean. You had so many plans together, and then there was that huge engagement party at the Graff."

"You're misunderstanding me. Sinclair was a fine kisser."

"Only fine?"

"His kisses were quite nice."

"That sounds even worse."

"No! They were nice. They made me feel lovely and safe. Protected."

"Like an expensive vase in a curio cabinet?"

"No. Yes." She frowned, frustrated. "My point is, he didn't take liberties."

"Not to be contentious, my sweet, but he also didn't marry you. Whereas, I did."

"Are you to be applauded? Should I open some champagne? What is your point?"

"That *I* didn't marry a glass vase. I married a woman. I married *you*."

Ellie was finding it increasingly difficult to follow the conversation, and she wasn't sure if it was because he was deliberately tripping her up, or if her brain was still addled from the kiss, because the kiss had warmed her from the inside out, making her feel so strange... so tingly and deliciously shivery.

She hadn't thought she'd like kissing him quite so much. She hadn't thought a kiss could be so... so... shattering.

Sinclair's two kisses had been sweet and respectful and, in hindsight, maybe too respectful, while Thomas's kiss hummed in her veins, making her feel wildly alive.

But was that a good thing?

She already had an impulsive nature. Was it right to feel so passionate?

Her brows pulled as she stared up at Thomas, trying make up her mind about him and the kiss and passion itself.

"What now?" he said dryly.

She couldn't tell if he was exasperated or amused, and did it matter if he was exasperated or amused?

His opinion wouldn't have mattered yesterday morning but everything was different now. He'd kissed her and she'd felt such wonderful and overwhelming things...

"Did you enjoy kissing me?" she blurted, before she could have second thoughts.

"Yes."

"If I hadn't stopped you, what would have happened?"

He smiled a faintly crooked, wicked smile. "I could show you."

"Not necessary!" She stepped back, bumping hard into the edge of the table. "I just wanted to know. So I could be prepared next time."

"Well, I'd keep kissing you and touching you, and I'd kiss not just your lips, but that little spot below your ear, and then your neck, and I'd find your breasts—"

"Okay, enough. Thank you."

"I'd put my hands beneath your skirt—"

"No more. I have a good picture now." She smiled tightly, and glanced away, her hands on her middle, holding the butterflies in.

His kiss had warmed her but his words had undone her. She felt excited and shocked and far too curious, heat rushing through her, making her skin burn from head to toe. Even her breasts felt full and aching, the stiff corset rubbing against her sensitive skin, chafing her. Tormenting her.

She was worried she'd like his hands on her breasts, and beneath her corset. But what if she didn't? And then, how would she manage him? How uncomfortable it would be between them then! "I realize men have an… appetite… but I really don't know you yet, and I think we need to become better acquainted before we kiss… and the rest of it."

"When will you be ready?"

"I don't know. It could be weeks… months…."

"Years?" he supplied helpfully.

"Maybe."

"Ah."

Something in his eyes made her look away and she knotted her hands. "But we have our whole lives ahead of us. Surely the… the… physical… isn't something we need to rush?"

"So no touching, just kissing?"

She was still not yet free of the effects of the earlier kisses. "Is kissing even necessary?"

"Yes. Kissing is necessary."

"Why?"

"Surely our marriage will include some affection?"

She squirmed inwardly at the way he said *some affection*, unsure which part she was more uneasy about, the word some, or the mention of affection. "All right. If you insist. One kiss a day, and I don't like it, but I'll do it as I acknowledge I have a wifely duty."

"I admire your strong sense of duty."

Her eyes narrowed. She was certain he was mocking her but he wasn't smiling, not that she could see. "You agree then? One kiss a day?"

"That's just impractical and downright stingy, Mrs. Sheenan. One kiss? You, ma'am, have no idea how hard I work for you—"

"Fine. Two kisses. That is it. That is all. Do not push. I'm already regretting agreeing to the second one."

"You do drive a hard bargain."

"You seem to be having a tremendous time at my expense."

"I'm just relieved we've agreed to the two kisses," he said gravely. "We have made substantial progress."

"Are you enjoying yourself?"

His dark eyes laughed at her. "Yes."

"Why?"

"You amuse me. I've never met anyone quite like you."

"No, I imagine all your other girls were quite smitten by

your dark hair and brown eyes and big frame. I'm sure they all wanted your kisses."

"Pretty much."

"Are you quite experienced?"

His broad shoulders shifted. "It depends on your definition of experience."

"Have you taken a woman to your bed before?"

"Yes."

"And done... everything?"

"Yes."

"Have you taken more than one woman to your bed?"

"Just to clarify, at a time, or..."

Her jaw dropped, and she flushed, going hot, then cold, and hot again. "You haven't!" she said breathlessly, heart racing, pulse drumming in her veins. She wasn't afraid, but overwhelmed by something far more complicated, and far more dangerous.

"I don't think this is a proper conversation, considering you are a proper young lady."

"And you are being deliberately provocative."

He had the audacity to smile, not just one of those faint wry smiles he'd perfected, but a wide, white smile that transformed his face, easing the hard jaw and strong cheekbones, and putting creases at his dark eyes.

It was all rather dazzling.

He was rather dazzling.

"I should go," he said, still smiling at her.

"Yes, you should," she answered tartly, thinking it was not fair that this husband of hers was so devastatingly handsome. "Goodbye."

And then he caught her by the waist and pulled her to him, hard, and his head came down and his mouth covered hers in another slow, hot kiss that made her melt on the inside and forget everything. Her mouth was his and she was his and she clung to him, needing the support as her legs threatened to give way.

"You're getting the knack of it," he said when he finally lifted his head. His voice was deep and rough and sent shivers through her.

She was still gripping his arms, her fingers wrapped around the warm dense muscle. "Now you've had your two," she said breathlessly. "You'll have to wait until tomorrow—"

He cut the words off with another kiss, the pressure of his mouth parting hers. His tongue traced her swollen upper lip and then found her tongue, teasing it, before sucking on the tip, the pulling sensation sending streaks of fire through her veins and heat low in her belly, matched by a bewildering new ache between her legs.

She shuddered as his hand brushed the side of her breast, and shuddered again when his knuckles brushed the taut peak, finding the straining nipple that her corset had chafed raw.

She shouldn't want this so much, and yet she did, and as his thumb found the nipple again, strumming it as though it were the strings of a violin, the heat beneath her skin made her frantic and breathless.

Ellie leaned into him, kissing him back, her hands gripping his arms and then, when that wasn't enough, she clung to his shoulders, fierce and hungry, but hungry for what she didn't know.

She was certain he knew, though, and she was certain he could answer this new feverish need. Just when she felt as if she'd burst out of her skin, he lifted his head, his dark gaze drinking her in. She couldn't look away, nor could she catch her breath.

She felt wild, and desperate and tricked. This was not just a kiss. This could not be called a kiss. A kiss is what Sinclair gave her. This was fiery and fierce and it flamed her senses and heated her blood and she'd never feel the same.

She'd never look at him the same.

Thomas lightly brushed her lips, sending yet another frisson of pleasure through her.

"Don't worry about making me anything for dinner, just concentrate on supper. I'll be hungry tonight. Don't disappoint me."

She blinked, surprised by the swift change of topics. "I'm not a cook!"

"You weren't a kisser, either, and now look at you." And he, the blasted man, *laughed* as he headed for the door.

ELLIE WATCHED HIM go, telling herself she was glad he was gone and, when she had to repeat it to herself, even more firmly the second time, she knew she was definitely in trouble.

THOMAS SMILED HIS entire way to the barn.

She was funny, this impetuous bride of his.

From the moment he met her, she'd been nothing but proud and prickly and fiercely independent.

She was high-handed, and stubborn, and nearly impossible, but he liked her fire. It matched her gleaming hair and her bright clear eyes that revealed everything she was feeling. She was painfully transparent and pathetically easy to torment and tease.

He shouldn't like tormenting and teasing her, but he did.

He liked the way her eyes widened and her lips parted before snapping closed. He liked the storms in her gaze as well as the dazzling light.

She was so alive. It was rather extraordinary to be near someone who felt so intensely. Her warmth was rubbing off on him. She was making him feel things he didn't think he'd feel again—laughter, lightness, pleasure, desire.

Maybe there was hope yet for him.

CHAPTER NINE

E LLIE BURNED THEIR supper.

It hadn't been intentional. She just wasn't very good at frying things, as the oil became quite hot and then started smoking and she didn't know how to keep turning the pieces of chicken so she wouldn't get burned from the splattering grease and the chicken would be rotated properly to cook all the way through before going black.

Mrs. Baxter had always made it look easy. Heat the oil, dredge the chicken in flour and salt and pepper and then put each piece in the oil and turn them every so often until the chicken was a nice golden brown, crunchy on the outside, and moist and tender on the inside.

Instead their chicken that night was a crispy black on the outside and pink and raw on the inside.

Thomas made a gallant effort to eat the chicken, too, but after two tentative bites, he took his plate, and hers, and carried them to the counter.

Without a word of criticism he cracked some eggs, whisking them, before cooking them in a smaller skillet to give them a quick, hot, edible supper.

Thomas hadn't made a fuss as he scrambled the eggs, and warmed slices of ham, and yet Ellie felt like a failure.

"I'm sorry," she said as Thomas pushed away his plate.

"There's nothing to apologize for," he answered.

"I told you I wasn't a cook."

"I wasn't, either, not until necessity forced me into the kitchen."

"When was that?"

"After my mam took ill."

It was on the tip of her tongue to ask another question but he'd abruptly risen and was stacking the plates, carrying them to the sink.

"I'll wash," she said, hating the uncomfortable knot inside her chest. "You take care of the things you still have to do today."

"I do need to look at the ledgers."

"I'm fine. Go to the parlor and do what you must do."

But instead of using the desk in the parlor or even the dining room like her father used to, he spread the books out on the kitchen table and made notes and scribbled numbers and calculated sums and periodically Ellie would glance at him as he worked, taking in how his big shoulders hunched and his head bent over the books.

She wondered if he was a little farsighted, or maybe he was just concentrating.

Either way, she couldn't stop watching him, keeping a closer eye on him than necessary, finding him a little too appealing sitting at the table, his chambray shirt sleeves rolled up to his elbows, the collar open at his throat, revealing far more of his chest than usual.

His skin was tan and smooth and every now and then she got glimpses of taut muscle. She felt a strange thrill looking at him, but the breathless tingle frightened her.

She wasn't afraid his mind-numbing kisses would ruin her, but that this new desire would change the dynamics with him, upsetting the already delicate balance between them.

If she wasn't careful, she'd want more from him, not less, which would give him more power over her. And with power came control.

She was already worried that he had too much control, and she'd been struggling these past few days with the fact that he'd quickly, easily stepped into her father's shoes, making the ranch his.

The way things were going, she'd also soon be his, and then who would she be?

What would happen to Ellie Burnett? Would she be gone forever, replaced by this new person called Mrs. Sheenan?

And yet it wouldn't be easy to resist him. She liked how she felt when he drew her into his arms. She liked how his touch stirred something in her, making her feel hot and fierce and wonderfully alive. After the months alone in her room, she welcomed the sensation of being so alive.

"I'm afraid I don't like your deals and agreements," Thomas said from the table, dropping his pen and stretching before leaning back in his chair and extending his legs. "I propose a new agreement, one that isn't about what you want, but what I want."

For a moment she didn't understand and then comprehension came. Heat washed through her and she nearly dropped the plate she was rinsing. "You mean, have... relations?"

"Why not consummate the marriage?"

Her face felt hot. She lifted a shoulder. What kind of question was that?

Instead she answered evasively, "I suppose because I'm not ready."

"You're afraid because you don't know anything about it. The physical side of the relationship is perhaps the easiest. It is certainly the most pleasurable. Far more pleasurable than arguing over how I manage Harrison, or how he should manage me."

She swallowed uncomfortably, her hot face now prickling. She didn't know what to say, and she didn't want to make eye contact any longer, but even staring doggedly into the sink, she could see him, his chiseled face all hard angles and planes, his mouth firm and quite kissable, his eyes that smoldering brown.

She'd thought him handsome that first night in front of the Graff Hotel, but he was even more appealing now, and not simply because of his looks, but because of his confidence and competence and the fact that he was somehow managing *her*. Quite spectacularly, too.

She darted a swift glance in his direction before focusing again on her skillet. "I don't think this is the right thing for us."

"Why not?"

"We still barely know the other—"

"I think we know each other surprisingly well."

"Perhaps from your point of view."

He chose not to respond to that. "I think after the first time, you'd be glad."

"I doubt it."

Her tart answer elicited a chuckle, the sound deep and rich, rumbling in his chest. "You're passionate, Ellie—"

"I'm not sure I understand the hurry, Mr. Sheenan," she interrupted, turning to look at him. "These things take time."

His eyes met hers and held. "We've been married for over three months."

"Let's revisit the topic in six months. Or better yet, a year. I promise to be more amendable then." She turned back to the sink and attacked the pan with focus and zeal, hoping he'd realize that the subject was closed. It was time for him to move on.

She heard his chair scrape back and then his footsteps on the floor. She sighed inwardly, aware that he was leaving, and she resented him for making her feel bad. They had an agreement. He might want to change the—

She lost her train of thought as she became aware of him standing right behind her.

Ellie bent her head and scrubbed the pan harder. *Don't make eye contact. Don't let him know you're flustered.*

He was so close now she could feel his warmth even without them touching. Her pulse quickened and her body tingled with awarencss. And then his head dipped and he kissed her lightly on the side of her neck.

She stiffened, resisting, but Thomas casually wrapped an arm around her waist and drew her back against him. Hot bright sparks shot through her and she sucked in a breath, feeling every place their bodies touched, and then he kissed her again, slightly lower on her neck, and even lighter, sending yet another shiver racing through her.

Ellie closed her eyes, feeling how her bottom pressed against his thighs, and how his hand splayed on her middle, his palm flat against her stomach, his warm fingers flexing, gently kneading.

Her legs trembled. She clutched the skillet handle. "I'm trying to do the dishes," she protested, voice low and husky.

He ignored her, kissing her neck again, finding another spot, this one just beneath her earlobe. "I'm not stopping you," he answered.

She closed her eyes as his lips lingered on the delicate sensitive hollow, heating her skin, the coolness of his lips sparking nerves that weren't just in her neck, but far below.

Ellie reached for the scouring pad, the rough metal grating her knuckles. "I can't concentrate on dishes when you do that."

"You're not trying very hard," he said, lips traveling down her neck, making her pulse beat wildly, recklessly. "Finish scrubbing the skillet."

"I can't."

His hand slid up her stomach, over her ribcage, stopping just under her breasts. She could feel the back of his fingers through her corset and bodice of her gown, and she could feel her breasts swell, straining in response.

She wanted him to press up against her breast, hoping that would ease the teasing, maddening sensation building inside.

"Try," he answered, lightly biting at her neck.

She gasped and leaned forward against the sink, hands bracing herself as pain and pleasure raced through her. She hadn't imagined a kiss or a touch could melt her, nor had she expected that a nip of his teeth would make her feel hot and wanton.

His palm covered her breast, his fingers finding her budded nipple, rubbing it through the fabric and then giving the taut peak a tug. Sensation streaked through her as bright lights flashed in her head.

"Finish," he insisted.

She wanted to turn in his arms and kiss him. She wanted

his arms around her and his mouth drinking her in, all of her, making her tingle, making her hum.

She'd never felt so many things before and it was wonderful and maddening, but mostly wonderful and if she could just have him hold her and satisfy this restless yearning feeling, satisfy the emptiness and the hunger. It wasn't just the physical craving, either, and it wasn't just curiosity, it went deeper than that. She felt more than that. She felt desperate to not just have his touch, but him, his hunger and his heart—

Ellie stiffened, drawn short by the thought.

It was a strange, bewildering thought.

She didn't want his heart. Why would she want him to love her? She didn't love him. She didn't even like him.

Or maybe she did like him, a little…

Or maybe she didn't like him, but simply desired him.

It was confusing. Too confusing. Suddenly her eyes burned and a lump filled her throat and she used an elbow to push him back. "I will be able to finish once you leave me alone." The words would have stung if her tone was sharp. Instead it was soft and broken.

THOMAS HEARD THE change in her voice, and it resonated more than the elbow to his ribs. Was she crying?

"You don't have to admit that you enjoyed yourself," he gently teased. "I won't tell anyone."

Ellie straightened, and made a soft sniffle sound. "You're far too confident of your abilities."

"Careful. I love a good challenge. Unless you're ready to end up in my bed tonight, I wouldn't throw the gauntlet down."

"Well then, no gauntlet thrown because the last place I want to be is your bed." She shot him a cool quick look. "For one, it's far too small."

Her eyes were wet and yet her lips quivered in a faint smile.

He didn't know if he wanted to kiss her or spank her, or both. She was so smart and sassy and beautiful and he wanted her mouth and wanted her naked and it was all he could do today to keep away from her.

She had no idea how much he wanted her.

She had no idea how much she tested his control.

"Why were you about to cry?" he asked.

"I wasn't."

And yet her voice was still husky and he wanted to know the truth. "But you did get upset."

She seemed determined to brush him off, and turn it into a joke. "When am I not upset? Papa used to say I was a regular powder keg, just waiting to explode."

He shifted to the side, and leaned against the counter next to her, so close that his hip brushed hers and he could see her face clearly.

It still wasn't dark yet outside, even though it had to be

close to nine. Thomas loved how long the days were in summer here. The long summer reminded him of home in the best sort of way.

"I like your emotions," he said.

"Ha!"

"I do. I have none, so it's good one of us feels something."

She looked up at him then, her green eyes wet. "Everyone has emotions. You just don't like to show them. It must be a male thing, because Papa was the same way."

"Perhaps it is a male thing," he said wryly. "And speaking of male things, I should go do my last check on the animals before securing the barn for the night."

But as he headed out, he glanced at Ellie, still at the sink. She was frowning down at her blackened skillet, lost in thought and he wondered what she was thinking. She hadn't told him why she was upset, effectively sidestepping his questions by mentioning her father. It had distracted him just enough for him to drop the subject, but he was concerned.

He might not be comfortable expressing his emotions, but he was equally uncomfortable being the source of her pain.

So what had made her teary tonight?

He wanted to understand so he could make sure not to do it again. They had made a good marriage, and were a good match, and there was no reason they couldn't enjoy each other. The physical would help cement their relationship, provided they could weather the emotional ups and downs.

ELLIE FOLLOWED THOMAS out the mudroom door and stood on the small back porch, chewing the inside of her lip, watching him stop at the corral and check the gate and before continuing on to the barn.

He was big and confident and nothing like her father, but somehow he'd stirred something in her, bringing her to life, and as he disappeared into the barn, the big door closing behind him, she felt a peculiar pang, that was bittersweet and perplexing.

She liked him.

In fact, her feelings were stronger than like. Her feelings were suspiciously strong, as though she'd had feelings for him all along...

As though she hadn't just noticed him that night in December in front of the Graff, but had fallen for him...

Was that why she'd been so sharp with him when he'd stopped to help her after her buggy incident, because instead of helping her, he'd chastised her?

And had she perhaps wanted to marry him, not because he was big and physically fit for the work, but because she was attracted to him, and didn't want to admit her feelings?

Ellie closed her eyes and then opened them, finally seeing

what she hadn't been able to see before.

She'd wanted Thomas from the beginning. She'd fallen for him right away, and had wanted him, and had convinced him to marry her, because he was the man she'd always wanted. He was the man her heart desired.

And if all that was true, then she'd lied to him when she'd married him. She'd told him she didn't want anything from him, and had no expectations of him...

Which was a lie.

She didn't just have expectations, she had hopes and dreams... dreams of being loved just as she loved him.

She loved him.

Ellie gulped a breath and held it, overwhelmed.

By acknowledging the truth, she'd just changed everything.

THE ACRID SMELL of charred meat greeted Thomas as he entered the house through the mudroom and he suppressed a sigh.

He was tired and hungry and he ached from head to toe thanks to being thrown across a horse stall by an irate black stallion.

Sitting down on the narrow bench in the mudroom, he tugged off one boot before gingerly working off the other, trying not to wince as he freed the throbbing foot.

He peeled off the sock and examined the swelling.

It wasn't pretty but he also didn't think any bones had been broken.

"What happened?" Ellie's voice came from the kitchen doorway.

He heard her concern and shrugged. "Nothing." There was no point worrying her, not when she was going to have to apologize to him for again burning dinner.

He didn't know why she found the basics of cooking so challenging. But maybe all women did. Or maybe it was because she didn't have a mother to teach her.

He didn't know, and he wasn't in the mood to be sympathetic when it was her horse who had bit him and then kicked him because Oisin was fed up with being trapped in his stall.

Thomas was fed up, too. He wanted supper, a proper supper, something filling that would appease his hunger and let him go to bed with a full stomach tonight.

"You've cut your cheek," she said, "and torn your shirt."

"I lost my footing," he said, trying to muster enthusiasm for more scrambled eggs and ham and hard flat biscuits when he craved fluffy mashed potatoes swimming with butter, and flavorful meat pie steaming hot out of the oven.

"You've been fighting," she said.

He rose and winced again. "Yes. And as you can see, I lost."

"Why did you get into a fight?"

"Ask your damn horse."

"Oh." She twisted her hands together. "I'm sorry."

"It's fine."

"No, it's not. I need to ride him."

"Yes, you do."

And then as he limped past her into the kitchen, she blurted, "I burned our steaks. I'm sorry. I shouldn't have been trying to do two things at one time."

"It's okay," he said, seeing the skillet with the two blackened strips of what appeared to be leather. Another completely inedible meal. He closed his eyes, battled for patience, and then opening his eyes he looked across the kitchen and stiffened.

The wall was gone. She'd removed all the boards he'd put up. Or she'd had someone remove the boards. The wall looked worse for the nail holes, too.

"I got busy and forgot to keep an eye on the steak," she said nervously. "I think the fire was too hot again."

As he turned to her, he saw how she laced her fingers, knitting them together. She was looking at him with worry and even a little bit of fear and he hated that. She didn't need to fear him. He'd never hurt her.

"I know you put the wall up," she said in a rush. "But it made everything harder for me, when I'm carrying laundry or trying to tidy the house, and so I thought it'd be nice if we just made the house attractive and open again, and that way if we do invite people over, our guests won't think we're having marital problems."

His forehead creased, torn between amusement and dismay. "Are we having marital problems?"

"Well, it hasn't been the most idyllic honeymoon. Papa's funeral and then I disappear for months and now we have to figure out how to get along."

"I think we're figuring that part out."

"Are we?"

"Mmmm." He glanced toward the kitchen opening with the battered trim. "That must have been a lot of work."

"It's fine. It was a good activity, finally had some proper exercise."

He was still hungry, and still bruised, but he was no longer in such a terrible mood. "How would you feel about going to town for supper? Would you be able to change quickly so we could eat tonight in Marietta?"

"It's not too late to go?"

"Not if we leave soon, and take your small buggy. It's been repaired and it should get us there quickly."

"Especially the way I drive."

"I think I'll drive, if you don't mind."

"Are you going to hitch Oisin, or should I?"

He made a rough sound in the back of his throat. "I think we'll let Oisin sit this one out and we'll take Crockett to town. He could get us there and back with his eyes closed."

"I'll go change."

"Can you grab me a clean shirt from my room on your

way down?"

She nodded and hurried up the stairs, but as she rushed away, Thomas saw her smile and her smile warmed him. It felt good to make her smile. She deserved to be happy. She deserved a man who'd cherish her, and spoil her a bit.

Ellie was back downstairs in just a few minutes, having changed into a butterscotch yellow dress with a bustle and fitted sleeves. The square neck had a delicate burgundy lace trim and there was a matching band of burgundy on the sleeves and hem. The yellow and red should have clashed with her vivid hair but instead she looked fresh and bright and perfectly elegant for a summer night's drive into town.

They were on the road, and had been traveling north for a good fifteen minutes before Ellie asked him if they were going to the Graff for supper.

He shook his head, the reins loose in one hand. Crockett was such a dependable horse. He needed little guidance. "I'm taking you to the diner on Main Street. I'm sure you've eaten there before."

"Actually, I haven't. Papa wasn't fond of the woman who owned it." There was laughter in her vice, and her smile was impish. "I think years ago he had a relationship with her, and when it ended, it ended badly. He couldn't ever speak of her without shaking his head and muttering things under his breath."

Thomas smiled. "Why do you think it ended?"

"I imagine she wanted him to marry her and when he

wouldn't, she broke it off, and then he was upset because I suspect he was quite fond of her."

Thomas cleared his throat. "You have quite an imagination."

"Papa was a romantic."

He glanced at her, expression mocking. "And you're not."

She colored and sat up straighter. "No. I'm practical." And then she averted her face and watched the passing scenery with intense interest, as if the landscape was all new to her.

They traveled for long minutes in silence. Thomas was smiling on the inside. Ellie amused him. Even when she wasn't trying to be funny, she still managed to make him laugh.

"Do you know what I'm ordering tonight at the diner?" he asked after a while, breaking the silence.

She was still staring out at the trees and shrubs lining the Yellowstone River. "Burnt steak? Undercooked chicken?"

The corner of his mouth curled. She was still annoyed with him. "Do you think those delightful options will be on the menu?"

"Well, they would be at home." Ellie looked at him, her spine straight, her green eyes flashing. "Incidentally, I can be practical, *and* romantic. Those two things aren't mutually exclusive."

He grinned at her. She was so fiery and fierce and oh,

how he wanted her. He was a physical man who expressed himself through touch. He didn't like words, and didn't trust words, but in bed he was able to communicate just fine. Now he just needed to get her into his bed and make her his. He ached to make her his.

Soon.

IT WAS A sleepy night in Marietta, and Ellie suspected that everyone was still probably worn out from the Fourth of July festivities the week before. She was tempted to ask if they could stop by Johanna's shop, but it was late and she didn't want to delay them in case the diner stopped serving supper anytime soon.

They were seated immediately in the café with the red brick walls and copper ceiling. There were big wooden booths lining the walls and then tables scattered in front of the huge plate glass windows.

The menu was written on a black chalkboard on the wall, and Thomas ordered the steak & stout pie and she chose the pan-friend trout. In the end, she wished she'd ordered the hearty meat pie, a dish of beef cooked with bacon, onions, mushrooms and a good dark beer, before being covered with a flakey crust and popped back into the oven until the crust was a mouthwatering golden brown.

Thomas gave her a bite of his supper, and it was flavorful and delicious. "I'll have to try to make this," she said. "But I suppose I need to get the recipe."

"Do you cook with recipes?"

"I haven't so far."

"Ah."

"I've tried to cook from memory but that hasn't worked out so well. I think having more specific directions might help," she said earnestly.

He grinned. "Perhaps."

"You'll have to tell me what your favorite meals are so I can try to make them. I will probably burn or ruin most, but at least you'll know I made the effort."

"To burn my favorite meals?"

She laughed out loud, eyes crinkling at the corners and for a moment Thomas couldn't breathe around the strange ache in his chest.

She was so beautiful. He didn't know what he'd done to deserve her, but now that she was his, he'd take care of her, and protect her as if his life depended on it.

And maybe it did.

ALTHOUGH SHE'D BEEN laughing, she'd also been watching Thomas closely and she saw the moment his expression changed, humor giving way to something more elusive and mysterious.

"Why did you marry me?" she asked.

He leaned back against the wooden booth. "Have you

ever looked at yourself in the mirror? You're the most beautiful woman in Marietta. Maybe the most beautiful woman in Montana."

She arched a brow, deliberately provocative. "So you married me for my face?"

He grinned lazily. "And the rest of it."

"And what does that mean? My property… my inheritance?"

"No, your figure."

She'd just taken a sip from her glass and she spluttered. "You have studied my figure?"

"Of course. If a man says he only wants you for your mind, you can rest assured he's lying."

Ellie set her glass down, both amused and delighted by his answer. Her father had always had a good sense of humor and she enjoyed the banter. "You admit you're shallow."

"Absolutely, irredeemably shallow."

She couldn't stop smiling as her gaze skimmed his face, and the relaxed way he sat back against the booth, as if the world, and everything in it, was his. "Did you expect me to be so much work?"

"I did."

"So you were prepared?"

"More than prepared." And the he paused, adding, "But in all fairness, you are not that much work."

There was something in his deep voice that made her insides tighten, putting a little flutter in her chest. "And yet I hate doing laundry," she said breathlessly.

"Is that why you've done none?"

"I've done some, just not a lot, and I will dust every few days, but I seriously doubt I'm ever going to get on my hands and knees to scrub the floors."

He sighed with exaggerated heaviness. "I suppose we could try to have Mrs. Baxter pop in now and then."

"What?" she cried in mock horror. "My punishment is being rescinded?"

"You weren't ever being punished. I was just trying to... motivate you."

"You wanted me out of bed and into the land of the living." Her shoulders twisted in a delicate shrug. "It worked. Here we are."

"Here we are," he agreed, lifting her hand to his lips.

She sucked in a breath as his lips brushed the back of her hand, sending rivulets of pleasure racing through her. He was so big and darkly handsome and he fascinated her far too much. Her feelings for him just kept getting stronger, and she wanted more from him, not less, which completely went against their agreement when they married. Their marriage was a business deal. It was a practical arrangement that would benefit both, and yet lately she was having the most impractical thoughts and feelings. And she was having so many feelings, too.

"Do you regret marrying me, Thomas?"

"No."

"You're sure?"

"Yes."

And then she couldn't think of anything else to say because her heart was beating fast and her thoughts kept scattering and all she could think was that she didn't just care for him a little bit. Oh no, when she did anything, she did it all the way, and she was head over heels in love with Thomas, and one day she hoped he would fall in love with her, too.

But then he shocked her by his brusque question. "Do you still miss him? Sinclair Douglas?"

She sat a little taller. "No."

"Your life would have been quite different if you'd married him."

"Yes, I would have lived on the Douglas property instead of my property."

"He was going to run both spreads?"

"I don't know. We never really discussed it, not in detail."

"But you were in love with him."

Her lips compressed. She glanced away, uncomfortable with the questions. What had she felt for Sinclair? It seemed like a lifetime ago. She couldn't even remember the attraction anymore.

"Papa knew him, and liked him. He was a good rancher. His property adjoins ours and he's been a good neighbor."

"I know you had feelings for him. That first night I saw you, out in front of the Graff Hotel, you were trying to stop him from getting into the fire wagon. You were frantic. You didn't want him to go. It was obvious how much you cared for him."

Her shoulders twisted. "But he didn't want me. He didn't love me. I don't know what else I can say."

ELLIE SAT CLOSE to Thomas on the way home, her arm tucked through his. It was strange to think that a week ago she was fighting him like an alley cat, and now all she wanted was to sit close and enjoy the ride home.

He smelled so good, and he made her feel safe and secure, which is remarkable since she hadn't expected to feel that way again, not after her father died.

"I'm glad Papa approved of you," she said, breaking the silence as the lavender light of dusk deepened to inky blue. "And I'm glad he was there when we married. It meant everything to me."

"And him."

She nodded a little. "I haven't been to his grave yet."

Thomas glanced at her. "Are you ready to go?"

A good question, one she had to think about. "Maybe not yet, but soon. At least to take him flowers." And then her voice broke and she bit down hard into her lower lip to keep from making a sound.

Thomas shifted the reins to one hand and slid an arm around her, bringing her even closer to his hip. "Grief takes time. Just when you think you're doing better, grief rises and pulls you back under."

She leaned against him, her head resting on his shoulder. "Did you go to the cemetery often, when you were in Ireland?"

"No. It was bad enough attending the funeral. I never felt the need to return just for the sake of visiting."

"If we ever go to Ireland, would you take me there?"

"To Rathkeale, or the cemetery?"

"Both."

"Not planning on going back, but if I did, I'd take you wherever you wanted to go."

"Promise?"

He gazed down into her eyes a long moment and he nodded once, a short decisive nod.

"Promise."

She reached up and cupped the back of his head, shyly drawing his face to hers to kiss him lightly on the lips. "Thank you," she whispered, before kissing him again.

IT WAS THE sweetest of kisses, Thomas thought, but not nearly enough, and he lifted her from the bench seat onto his lap.

Her eyes widened with surprise and she put a hand out to brace herself against his chest. "Is this safe?"

"Probably not if you were driving, but you're not, I am,

and Crockett knows his way home." And then lowering his head, Thomas covered her mouth with his.

He felt her quick inhale, and then she sighed, her lips parting for him, her body shaping to his.

His lips traveled slowly over hers, savoring the lush softness of her mouth. She tasted of the peaches and cream they'd had for dessert, and he wanted to eat her, all of her. He'd been with many women, but only Ellie made him feel like this—fierce and carnal and oh, so protective.

He'd kill for her, and die for her, without even giving it a second thought.

She was his, and he was put on earth to protect her, and all he wanted now was to feel her and hold her and lose himself in her.

She trembled in his arms as he deepened the kiss, his body hardened further. "Do you have any idea how much I want you?" he ground out roughly.

"I have an idea," she whispered.

"I want you like I've never wanted any woman, Ellie. And I might not be the husband you wanted—"

"But you are," she interrupted. "You're exactly the one I wanted."

CHAPTER TEN

H E SLEPT WITH her in her room that evening, although sleeping was probably not the correct term as what they did together wasn't sleeping, nor could she sleep after.

As she lay awake afterward, she replayed the evening, still rather awed and even a little bit overwhelmed. They'd consummated the marriage and she was no longer a virgin. And physical relations were nothing like she'd expected. After the initial awkwardness, and discomfort, it was really quite nice. More than nice. It was like the pleasure of kissing times one hundred.

Make that a thousand.

Ellie hadn't thought she would be surprised by his body, having seen pictures and books, not real men of course, but Greek statues and so forth, but Thomas nude was quite different than Michelangelo's famous David. For one, Thomas was taller, and bigger, everything was bigger from his shoulders to his legs. There were more muscles and a smaller waist and there was the matter of his manhood.

His masculine proportions put poor David to shame.

At first sight, Ellie had been sure that an erect Thomas

was far too large for her. There would be no way her body could actually accommodate his, but it seemed that Thomas's expertise meant she didn't just accommodate him, but he knew how to make sure she also enjoyed him, and she had.

Now that she understood the mechanics of the act, she looked forward to trying it again because this next time she would be less nervous and more able to focus on the exciting sensations, especially that climax at the end where her body felt like it had become one of those fireworks shot from behind the courthouse on Montana's day of statehood last November.

The sensation of him in her had been astonishing and, once the first pain went away, she'd been surprised by the lovely warmth of it all, and how much she'd loved being beneath him, and how he'd kissed her as he filled her. That delicious pleasure just grew, too, and she knew somewhere in the back of her brain that he was controlling the whole thing, the tempo, the connection, and just when she was breathless, just when she thought it couldn't get better, she shattered as though exploding in the sky, before gently falling in glittering lights.

Afterward, she was sticky and sore, and Thomas went downstairs, returning with a cool damp cloth to put between her legs. She felt awkward and shy as he tried to wash her and she pulled the cloth away. "Let me do that!"

He grinned at her embarrassment. "I'm afraid I've taken your virtue, Mrs. Sheenan."

"You did a good job of it, too," she flashed, shooting him a mischievous look as she lay back down next to him. And then she winced. She was still surprisingly sore.

"It will be sore for a day or so," he said. "But it shouldn't ever hurt that much again. The first time is the worst."

"You specialize in virgins, Mr. Sheenan?"

"No. But I have a conscience. I don't want to ever hurt anyone, much less a woman."

"How is it you've been with other virgins and you haven't married them?"

He rolled onto his back, arms behind his head. "I intended to marry one, but her father wouldn't approve of the marriage."

"Did you tell her father you'd compromised her?"

"Never. He would have taken it out on her."

"Where was that?"

"In Rathkeale."

"How old were you?"

"Eighteen, or nineteen."

"Why didn't her father approve?"

"She was English. I was Irish."

Ellie processed that for a bit. Her mother's family was Irish. They'd been here far longer than Thomas but she couldn't imagine that Ireland was so different seventy-five years ago. "Was she wealthy?"

"I don't know if she was. But her father had land."

"An aristocrat?"

"Close enough."

Ellie chewed on her lip, thinking of this girl he'd wanted but couldn't have. "What if she got pregnant?"

"There are ways to reduce the risks of pregnancy."

"Did we do that tonight?"

"No."

Ellie's eyebrows rose. Until this moment she hadn't even thought about conception, or having a child. She wasn't ready to be a mother. She wasn't even comfortable being a wife yet.

He sat up and looked down at her. "Are you concerned about getting pregnant?"

"I want children. I'm just not sure I'm ready yet." She reached up and touched the back of his arm, fingers exploring the hard, bunched tricep. "I don't feel like I even know you yet."

"Whatever happens, it'll be fine," he said firmly, with a confidence she didn't feel.

But she nodded and drew the sheet up to cover herself.

He stopped her, his hand parting her thighs, his torso bending over her. She wasn't sure she needed more help from him, but then he kissed the inside of her thigh, and kissed her right over her curls, and then the tip of his tongue found the silken nub he'd stroked so cleverly before.

She gasped and tried to push him away but he held her knees open so that he could take his time kissing her where she was so very sensitive. Ellie couldn't breathe. Her heart raced and her body melted as he licked and kissed until she was soon sobbing his name as she shattered all over again.

Now she lay dazed and spent, her body so warm that she couldn't even imagine pulling the sheet over her. But then, it didn't help having a mammoth of a man in bed next to her, especially when the bed wasn't particularly large.

They'd need to sort out the bed situation one of these days. She couldn't imagine taking over her father's room. Could they just get a bigger bed for her room?

"Stop thinking," a gruff Thomas muttered, reaching out to pull her closer to his side.

She turned her head to look at his face. He was big and tough out of bed, but in it, he was sensitive, skillful, and devoted to her pleasure. "I'm jealous of the women you've loved before me."

"Don't be. I married you, not them."

"But you must have made them all feel this way."

"No." He kissed her forehead. "Now no more talking. We need to sleep," he added, his hand sliding down her waist, to stroke her hip. "Morning will be here soon."

"That's right. You have to work."

"And what will you be doing, Mrs. Sheenan?"

"Sleeping in. Relaxing. Just enjoying my bed."

He opened his eyes and looked into hers, his dark gaze heavy lidded, his black lashes concealing his expression. "You know what will happen if I find you in bed."

She smiled faintly. "Promises, promises."

He gave her backside a light spank, and then rubbed her cheek where it was warm. "Careful, I'm hard again and you need to recover." And then he pulled her backside against his hips, and he was indeed hard, his erection pressing against the cleft of her bottom, and she held her breath, afraid to wiggle because her nerves were already dancing, making her aware there were still so many things she didn't know. She just hoped Thomas would be patient and teach her.

And then finally, somehow, she did fall asleep, and when she woke up the next morning, Thomas was gone.

FOR ELLIE, THE next week passed in a blur of wildly contradictory emotions and seductive sensation.

It didn't take her long to get used to having Thomas in her bed, although the pleasure wasn't just the physical, but him. He was always different after they made love. He'd tell her things she didn't think he'd ever share otherwise, and she took advantage of his openness when they were lying in bed together, wanting to know everything she could about him so they could become closer, and even more intimate.

Thomas, she'd noticed, was good with touch and giving her pleasure, but during the day he had a tendency to withdraw. It was odd, but the more passionate they were in bed, the cooler he seemed to be during the day. She hoped it was just her imagination, but couldn't be sure because so much was changing, including making love. It was rarely the same. Every time she thought she understood the basics, the basics changed. It seemed that there wasn't just one way to make love, but rather a dizzying number of positions and variations—on top, on bottom, on one's knees, on one's side, sitting up on his lap...

She thought she liked most of them, although there were a few where she felt awfully exposed, especially if they were doing them in the afternoon, after dinner before he returned to work. He liked her to straddle his hips and "ride" him, and while she liked how it felt, she did feel naked on top.

Perhaps because she was naked, when sitting on him. But still...

They'd just spent the past hour in bed, and she knew from the past week, that he'd soon be leaving her, and dressing again and heading out.

She wasn't ready for him to go. She was lonely when he was gone, and she felt anxious and empty until he returned and kissed her again, and made her feel wanted again.

Maybe that was the problem. She only really felt wanted when he was touching her. Lately, when he did his books, or tackled simple repairs in the evening, he didn't look at her or try to talk to her. He just focused on his task and she tried to find things to do to keep herself busy, things that would keep her from thinking about them, and how Thomas felt about her.

They weren't a love match. He'd never promised her love, and she told him that she wasn't expecting romance or even affection, and so she'd set herself up for disappointment.

It didn't help that every time he kissed her, or his body covered hers, she fell even more deeply in love. Making love only intensified her emotions, making her crave him and his skin and the intimacy of being wanted by him.

She'd tried to tell him how she felt, but the last time she'd mentioned the word "feelings" he'd shut down and climbed from bed, and she didn't want that to happen today.

Rolling onto her side, she studied his profile. He was staring at the ceiling, one arm behind his head, his black brows a strong clean slash above his straight nose and firm mouth.

"Tell me more about you," she said, placing a hand on his chest.

He tensed and she lightly circled the spot above his heart. "I know you don't want to talk about your family," she said, keeping her tone as light as her fingertips, "but can you talk about your home, where you grew up?"

"There is very little to tell. We didn't have much. You'd be disappointed. We weren't anything special."

"Knowing you, I don't believe that is true."

He made a soft mocking sound that made his chest rumble. "I think all the pleasure has gone to your head."

She smiled crookedly. "Maybe, and maybe not. I can't help being curious about you. After all, I will need stories to tell our children."

"Our children won't need to know about Ireland—"

"Nonsense. I love Ireland."

"You've never been."

"My mother's people loved it, too."

"Then why did they leave?"

She rolled her eyes. "I'm not asking for your deepest, darkest secrets! I just want to know more about you. Isn't there anything you can share? A little morsel to amuse me? You know so much about my life here. I just want to know more about your life before I met you."

He was silent a moment, and then he reached over and smoothed her hair back from her face, stroking the long red tendrils behind her ear and then down over her shoulder. "There is one thing. I haven't told anyone this, and I'm not sure what you will think, but it's amusing. At least to me."

"Tell me."

"Until I came to America, my surname wasn't Sheenan, but Sheehan. It changed when I went through immigration. The official at Ellis Island wrote it down wrong and I don't know if he was irritated, or not feeling well, but when I pointed out the error, he said maybe America didn't need another smart mouth, and so I told him never mind. Sheenan was a good name and I was on my way. And for the past six years Sheenan has been a good name."

"But it's not your real name," she cried.

"It's not such a big deal—"

"It is!"

He shrugged. "Sheehan is a common name where I'm from. You'll find Sheehans all over County Clare and Limerick, although you'll get different spellings. Sheahan, O'Sheehan and O'Sheahan. Now I just have one more variation."

"But it's not your proper name! Why wouldn't you insist he fix it?"

"It would have been a long, expensive trip home."

"But were you not proud of your surname, because I loved Burnett? I loved being my father's daughter."

"The O'Sheehans were a really old family in Ireland. They dated back to the tenth century, and were a powerful clan in the old days, but the O'Sheehans, like most of the Irish clans, suffered following the British invasion. Cromwell and his men stripped the Irish clans of their land and property giving them to English settlers. Our clan, like others, lost virtually everything, turning us into peasants in our own country, and we've been peasants ever since. I'm sure that's why your mother's people left, too."

Her mouth opened, then closed. She gave her head a confused shake. "I just think one's name is so important."

"I agree. But maybe this was a good thing. I'd begun to feel as if my family was cursed. Maybe being Thomas Sheenan has changed my luck. In fact, I know it has. I married you."

"But your family—"

"They're all gone, and the only family that matters now

is ours."

Ellie drew a slow breath but found it hard to relax. Even with her eyes closed, her heart continued to beat too hard. "That is a terrible story," she whispered.

"I think it's rather funny."

"How is it funny?"

"I just keep thinking, how many other names did that irritated, or sickly, agent misspell? How many others are living in America with a different name because the immigration official couldn't be bothered to get it right?"

"You're just making me more upset!"

"Don't be upset, or I can't tell you any more stories when you ask."

"Hmph."

Thomas kissed her then to distract her, and then he held her, loosely, easily, until she fell asleep and now he watched her nap, her thick auburn hair spilling over her arm and across her pillow.

This afternoon he'd had her once, twice, and he should be satisfied, but he still felt restless, heavy with a need he couldn't assuage.

He'd never known such desire. He'd never known such hunger.

He told himself it was because he'd gone almost a year without a woman, but in his heart, he knew that wasn't it.

He was becoming attached to her, maybe too attached.

The emotion wasn't comfortable. It made him worry

about her, and feel possessive, and even more responsible. Yes, she was his responsibility, just the way the land and the livestock were in his care, but he couldn't get soft. He couldn't allow his emotions to rule his head. Life was hard enough without emotions clouding one's thinking.

He leaned over her, brushed her lips with his, breathing in her smell and the warm softness of her skin and then because he had already dallied too long, he left the bed and quietly slipped into his trousers and then grabbed his shirt and boots.

He had to rethink these lazy afternoons with her, no matter how lovely.

Maybe he had to rethink it all.

THOMAS SPOKE TO her at supper, letting her know that he wouldn't be coming back to the house after dinner, and that once he left in the mornings, he'd be gone until late.

Ellie had known all throughout the meal that something was bothering him. He'd been even quieter than usual and he hadn't smiled at her once, or looked into her eyes, or paid her any attention other than thanking her for passing this, or serving that.

She chewed on her lip for a long minute, gathering her courage before asking, "Did I do something earlier—"

"No."

And yet, he'd cut her short in a hard, cold voice. Ellie

drew a quick breath, trying not to be hurt. "Are you angry because I made you talk about home?"

"No."

"I fell asleep and everything was fine, but you've been so cold ever since you came home this evening. It's almost as if you hate me."

He sighed impatiently. "I do not hate you."

"But you don't love me," she said in a small voice.

He shot her a swift, hard look. "Love was never part of the equation, Ellie, and you know it."

"Why can't it be?"

"Because I'm not that man. I'm not going to ever be that man."

"What does that even mean?"

"It means I am who I am—"

"You're not even trying!"

"You don't think I'm trying? You don't think I'm showing you any respect, any tenderness—"

"That's not what I mean. I just feel like you want lovemaking, but not really me."

"Who am I making love to then if it's not you?"

She bit down and looked away, blinking hard to keep her eyes from watering. "You know what I mean," she whispered.

"Sweetheart, this is who I am. This is what I am. If you're not happy, I'm sorry, but I've given you everything I can."

Her head dropped and she closed her eyes, holding the hurt in.

"I'm not in the mood for tears," he said roughly. "They're not going to move me."

"Just go away."

"I knew this would happen." He threw down his napkin and rose from the table. "I knew it wouldn't be enough for you. I'm not the kind of man you were dating. I'm not Sinclair Douglas, either. I'm not tender, or romantic, and I sure as hell won't write you poems—"

"I don't want poems. I don't even like poetry. It's annoying. But you... you're even more annoying right now. You're changing the meaning of my words!"

"You're the one that said you feel empty, and that this relationship feels empty. I'm sorry about that. I'm sorry you're disappointed, but I have tried to show you I will always take care of you, and protect you. I've tried to be a good husband, and fulfill my responsibilities, but if you're not satisfied, I don't know what else to do."

"But I don't want to be a responsibility! I don't want to be another duty. I want you to want me—"

"I do. When do I not reach for you at night? How have I left you dissatisfied in bed?"

She flushed. "You are very good in bed."

"So what is your complaint?"

Her mouth opened, and then closed without making a sound. "There isn't one," she said finally, eyes gritty and hot, as a lump filled her throat.

"Good," he snapped, before walking out.

Ellie cleared the table and did the dishes and then changed into her nightdress. She sat on the front porch in the rocking chair Thomas had brought out for her earlier in the week because it was cooler outside at night than in the house during the middle of July.

She rocked slowly, trying to soothe herself, not wanting to be upset, or cry. He didn't like it when she cried. He'd told her before that tears were a trick women used to get their way. It had made her angry at the time, but she'd never forgotten what he'd said and she was determined she'd be calm when he returned to the house.

He took his time returning, too, but at last she heard his boots inside the house, and then his footsteps on the stairs. He went up and then he came back down and opened the front door.

"I was looking for you," he said, joining her on the porch and leaning against one of the big log posts.

"It's nice out here. It's cool and the stars are so bright."

He said nothing and she touched the tip of her tongue to her upper lip. "I like it when we're together, Thomas, whether it's the afternoon, or at night. You always know how to pleasure me."

He just stared out over the landscape.

She pressed her nails into her hands, trying not to be nervous, wanting so very much to make him understand.

"But afterward it feels so different. It's as if you've pulled away—"

"But I haven't. I'm still lying there next to you."

Her eyes burned, the salty sting making her want to blink. "I don't mean in bed, Thomas. I mean once we're both dressed. Something in you seems to change. Like tonight at supper, and even now. It doesn't seem like you are the same with me. It's almost like you become someone else." Her voice faded and she held her breath, waiting for him to answer.

"I haven't," he said at length. "For better or worse, it's still me."

She didn't know what to say next, wasn't even sure if he wanted her to say anything. The silence stretched. It wasn't a comfortable silence, either. Knots formed in her stomach. Her nerves felt stretched to a breaking point.

"It's going to be an early morning for me," he said, still staring out at the moon washed valley. "We're moving the cattle up the mountain tomorrow. We'll be gone a couple days. A week at the most. I'll be back once they're settled."

She noticed he wasn't looking at her. He was doing everything he could to avoid meeting her gaze. "I remember those trips," she said quietly. "My father used to take me."

She paused, waiting for him to include her, wanting him to want her. But he said nothing and she felt a sharp lance of pain. It wasn't her imagination, he was shutting her out.

She didn't understand it, didn't know what was happening between them but he was pulling away and putting up a wall that hadn't been there before.

He finally broke the silence. "I'll be leaving early in the morning, probably before you're up."

She closed her eyes and held her breath, holding the pain at bay. He said he liked her emotions but she knew he didn't like her emotions when she was tearful or demanding. "I'll see you off," she said as cheerfully as she could.

"No need. Sleep in—"

"What if I'd rather get up to see you off? What if I want to say goodbye?"

"I'm not trying to quarrel, Ellie. I just thought you might enjoy sleeping in since we've had a number of... late nights."

What was going on? Why was he being so hard and distant? She didn't know where everything had gone wrong. The warmer he was in bed, the colder he was out of it. "Why do I feel like you're running away from me?"

He made a low, rough scoffing sound. "That's foolish."

Even his tone was sharp and hurtful. She struggled to smash her pain. "So you're not trying to escape me? Or avoid me?"

"No."

"Then why not invite me on the drive? Let me help. I'm a better cowhand than half those boys."

"It's no place for a woman."

"My father thought it was."

It was the wrong thing to say because his features hardened and his dark eyes narrowed. "But your father isn't here, is he? I'm here, and I'm not comfortable having you on the trail, much less a steep trail with five hundred head of cattle." He drew a short, rough breath before softening his tone. "I don't want to worry about you, Ellie, and I would. You're safer here at the house. I've got some of the hands staying down here, too, and they'll be keeping an eye on things as well."

"Now who is the one treating me like a glass vase in a curio cabinet?"

"My job is to protect you, Ellie—"

"Then stay here and don't go. If you're that worried about my safety, stay with me and protect me instead of leaving me for a week in the care of another man. Unless the issue is that you don't want me anymore, and if that's the case, just say so!"

"I don't have the time or patience to argue with you. I gave you my answer, I'm not going to change my mind. You're not going. I want you here—"

"Even if I don't want to be here?"

"It's not up to you, Ellie. It's my decision and I've made my decision. I need to turn in, but you know I won't go to bed until you're inside and everything is locked up tight."

"You're just going to go to bed now? Even though you know I'm so upset?"

"God, I could use a drink right now," he muttered.

"My father has a half dozen decanters in the parlor. All

kinds of whiskeys and port and brandy. Go drink yourself silly."

"Married to you, it wouldn't be hard to embrace the drink, and then I wouldn't worry so much about doing the right thing, or saying the right thing. I wouldn't care about self-control. Instead I argue with you, and fight with Harrison every time he lets me know I'm not doing something right, and then when I've had enough here, I could go to town and drink all day at Grey's Saloon, too, and then I could stagger out onto Main Street, taking our troubles public."

"And how would that help?"

"Because that way everyone would pity you. Poor Ellie Burnett, married to that useless Irishman."

"I've never said that, and I certainly don't want anyone to pity me."

"But you pity yourself, don't you?"

"Don't think you can sleep in my room tonight. You may return to your room. You're not welcome in mine."

"Is that how this is going to go?"

"You've stripped me of all my control. This is the only power I have left."

"Well then, by all means, use it, Mrs. Sheenan," he answered bitingly.

Chin high, she entered the house and stood stiffly in the hall as he locked the front door behind her. They climbed the stairs not speaking, and she went to her room and he went to his old room for the first time in over a week.

Ellie tried to hold on to her anger, needing it to protect her, needing the fury and hurt for strength, but she couldn't sleep and couldn't relax and couldn't distract herself, either. She missed her father. She missed his steadiness and his love.

Thomas didn't want her love. He wanted her body, but not her heart.

She wouldn't cry, though, and she made herself lie still, even though her eyes burned and her throat ached from all the pent emotion.

When her door opened a little later, she grabbed her pillow and threw it at the door. It hit Thomas in the chest before bouncing off the door. "You're not welcome here, Mr. Sheenan!"

"What about a truce?"

"No. I'm still mad at you."

"What if I can make you forget you're mad?"

"That won't happen."

"You're not even giving me a chance," he said, approaching the bed. He leaned over and kissed her, even as he stroked her hip, and then up.

He kept kissing her and touching her until she forgot about everything but him, and how much she cared for him, and how much she wanted to be with him, until she woke up the next morning and discovered Thomas gone.

WAKING UP TO discover that Thomas had left for the week without saying goodbye, crushed her. If he'd shut her out because she'd been rude, or ungrateful, or selfish she could understand. But to push her away because she wanted him?

Because she *cared* about him?

Her eyes stung and she wrapped her arms across her middle to keep from picking something up and throwing it.

He didn't understand that she'd never tried harder to please anyone. She'd never tried so hard to be a good woman, and what she hoped was a proper wife.

She'd tried to cook and set a pretty table. She'd gathered flowers and put them in glass jars and even tried to make his favorite dessert. And he'd been fine with all that. He was fine with the hot meal and the nice table and the not-perfectly-set fruit tart and then making love after. But that was all he wanted from her. She could cook for him, and clean for him, but she was not to have feelings. Not to care.

And she was most definitely not to ask *him* to care.

She should have just moved into the house on Bramble. She could have had a housekeeper and a gardener and more gorgeous clothes than she knew what to do with. Even better, she would have her independence, and complete financial freedom.

No interfering, arrogant husband to give her orders.

No irritating Irishman to drag her to bed.

No beautiful but impossible man to call her own.

No one to love.

And how she loved Thomas, which was what made it all so much worse.

Heartsick, she went to the mudroom door and stepped out on the porch to look up at Emigrant Peak. Thomas was up on that mountain somewhere. He and Harrison and a half dozen men were driving the herd, and it was a big herd this summer. They could have used her help. It would have been fun to get out there and ride again, and prove her worth again. She'd spent too many months in the house and she'd lost a little bit of herself this spring—

Ellie grimaced. She wasn't *that* interested in moving cattle. She wanted to be on the mountain because her handsome, irritating, impossible husband was there. And maybe it wasn't a place for most women, but she wasn't most women, she was his woman. She loved him. And wherever he was, she wanted to be.

Ellie stared at the peak another moment before turning away. It was too late to head up now, but at first light tomorrow, she and Oisin would be on their way.

CHAPTER ELEVEN

OUT ON THE trail leading toward the mountain, Thomas finally felt as if he could breathe again.

He'd felt suffocated for the past few days, trapped in a situation that threatened to only get worse, not better.

He hoped that distance from Ellie would give him perspective and a chance to clear his head.

And yet with a whole day in the saddle ahead of him, he had nothing but time on his hands, and his thoughts returned to her again and again. She was always there in his mind, and just remembering her quick eager smile made his chest grow tight. In the last week she'd become so full of warmth and light, and the happier she was, the guiltier he felt.

She deserved more. She deserved a man who'd love her properly, a man who had wooed her and won her, fighting hard for her. A man who'd say the things she'd want to hear, and put her first, and give her tenderness, not just hot carnal sex.

He was good at sex. But the other stuff… it wasn't him. It would never be him and she needed to accept facts or she'd be perpetually disappointed.

ELLIE LEFT A note for the men who'd remained behind, letting them know that she was with Thomas and all was well, and then after saddling Oisin, she set off for Emigrant Peak, leaving early to make the most of the cool morning.

As she reached the foothills she felt excited, as well as a little bit nervous. She really hoped that once she reached the camp, Thomas would be glad to see her. She didn't expect instant jubilation, but once the shock wore off she wanted him to be glad she'd made the effort and joined him. He needed to realize that she hadn't been born in an Irish village. She didn't need to be fussed over and protected. Ellie knew she was an excellent horsewoman as well as an experienced hand, and she'd grown up with tremendous independence on the ranch, and with that independence came responsibility.

Her father had insisted she be as skilled as any boy and so she'd been taught how to read animal tracks and be alert as to the wildlife around her. She'd learned about the weather in the valley and how to differentiate the clouds, and know which predicted storms.

But as the hours passed and she and Oisin continued to climb, her excitement gave way to unease. He wasn't going to be happy, was he?

Ellie's stomach churned, making her queasy. She ought

to go back home. She ought to turn around but the more worried she became, the more determined she was to prove to Thomas that he shouldn't have excluded her because she wasn't just a pretty face, but as hardworking and knowledgeable as any of the ranch hands.

She'd driven cattle through streams, rivers, scrub brush and ravines and she wanted to be there, at Thomas's side, so they could drive the cattle together.

She'd wanted a partnership. Someone who would let her be her. Someone who appreciated how much she loved the land, and her history on this land.

Last summer her father had been too ill to drive the cattle to the high pastures, but he'd done it every other year before and she'd been on each of those trips with him.

The work could be hot and miserable, but there was also beauty in the drive. The whispering aspens, the fragrant summer grass, the breathtaking views from the higher elevation. And she wanted to share it with him. She wanted to share all of life with him.

He had to understand that she was more than a woman, and she was certainly not fragile. She wasn't going to get sick and die, either, and she couldn't help wondering if that was his fear. He'd lost so many of his sisters, and maybe he even blamed himself.

Ellie sighed and pushed back her hat, today wearing her father's beloved straw one. She'd worn it as much for nostalgia as for courage.

She sighed again, fidgeting unhappily in the saddle as a little voice whispered inside her that she was maybe making a mistake. What if Thomas wasn't happy to see her? What if he was irritated that she'd gone against his wishes?

But why should he be irritated? Why shouldn't he include her? This ranch was her life, her land, her heritage. It's how she knew herself, and it was also a connection to her father. Being left behind, much less left behind in a house, would never make her happy.

HARRISON'S LOW WHISTLE caught Thomas's attention and Thomas glanced at the older man and saw him pointing toward the horizon.

Thomas narrowed his eyes against the bright afternoon sun, staring hard into the distance until he saw what Harrison had wanted him to see.

And then he couldn't believe his eyes. He stared hard at the horse and rider, jaw tight, molars grinding together.

Even with the hat, he recognized her, but it wasn't hard to recognize her, not on that huge black horse. Oisin was not a trail horse. He was meant for smart buggies, gently undulating meadows and well-paved roads. His height and long elegant legs made him particularly unsuitable for the narrow path that zigzagged up the mountain.

He knew that Harrison and the ranch hands were watching him, waiting to see what he would do. He disliked being put in that position, of having to rebuke his wife in front of employees, but he wasn't about to welcome her with open arms. He wasn't about to welcome her at all. This trip was no place for Ellie, and he made that abundantly clear.

In fact, he couldn't have been clearer if he tried, which meant Ellie didn't care what he thought, nor did she respect him.

THOMAS WASN'T HAPPY. He wouldn't even look at her. Ellie pretended to be oblivious, kicking her foot free of the stirrup, and then shifting her skirts to jump down from the saddle.

She landed lightly on her feet and Mr. Harrison approached, offering to take Oisin and have him fed and watered and rubbed down. She thanked Mr. Harrison and then peeled off her gloves and asked if Mrs. Harrison needed help with dinner.

"She might," Mr. Harrison answered noncommittally. "Check in with Mr. Sheenan and if he has nothing for you, you might see if my missus could use the help."

The last thing Ellie wanted to do was speak to Thomas now. She could feel his fury from across the camp. But she couldn't put Mr. Harrison in the middle. She nodded and headed toward Thomas, heart beating too hard.

She saw Thomas glance at her and then he averted his face as she approached. "Hello," she said, voice not entirely steady. "Surprise."

He said nothing.

She laced her fingers together. "I know you didn't want me to come, because you didn't think I could handle the drive, but you're wrong. I'm able to help, and I made it here easily. Yes, it's a long ride, but Oisin handled the trail beautifully. We had no accidents and no problems—"

"But if you had a problem, or an accident, what would you have done?" he interrupted tersely. "Who would have come to your aid?"

She counted to five, and then to ten. "But there were no problems. See? All in one piece. Good as new."

He shook his head and walked away from her, going to speak to Mr. Harrison about who knew what.

ELLIE PERCHED ON a rock and tried to stay out of Thomas's way, hoping that if she gave him some time, he'd calm down.

The horses were tied to the aspen trees, while the huge cattle herd was resting and grazing in the clearing. They were only halfway to the high pasture but this was where her father and Mr. Harrison always stopped for the first night since there was water in the small valley and plenty of shade, too.

Restless, Ellie finally tracked Thomas down. He was standing, talking to some of the hands, his back to her.

She approached, tapping him on the back. "I'm going to pick some berries over by the stream. Just wanted you to know so you didn't have to worry."

His dark head inclined. "Fine."

Her fingers balled into fists. She was so nervous and unsettled. She hated it like this. She hadn't come all this way for him to be so angry.

"Want to keep me company?" she asked quietly, hopefully, trying to smile but not sure it was the brightest or most confident.

It took him forever to reply and when he did, his answer was curt. "Sure."

He didn't look at her, though, as he walked next to her to the reach the wild tumble of vines growing along the stream, but she looked at him, and in the long, golden rays of afternoon sun, he looked glorious.

The breeze caught at his pale blue chambray shirt, pulling it away from his shoulders and giving her a tantalizing glimpse of bronze skin and his broad, muscular chest. Her fingers itched to touch his skin, and her lips tingled, aching for a kiss. Instead, she crouched next to the vines and began picking the wild blackberries. Every summer she picked them when she was here, turning most over to Mrs. Harrison for her famous cobbler, but also eating as many of the sweet-tart fruit as she could.

"I've always wondered who planted the first vine," she said, gently dumping a handful of berries in a corner of her skirt since she didn't have a basket.

Thomas looked at her and then away, jaw jutting with displeasure.

She glanced at his hard profile and then quickly back at the dark green vines, trying to focus on the purple black fruit. "I discovered these as a little girl," she continued. "They die every winter and then come back every summer. Over the years, the bush has grown considerably from just a few vines to this wild patch."

She kept her hands moving as she talked, determined not to take his silence personally, determined not to let him see how much he was hurting her. She didn't understand him at all. She didn't understand how he imagined his silence helped the situation.

When she'd collected a generous pile of berries, enough for Mrs. Harrison's cobbler, she stood, careful not to lose any of the berries as she shifted the apron she'd made from her long skirt.

"I'm going to take these to Mrs. Harrison," she said lightly. "Want to walk with me?"

He shook his head. He didn't even glance her way. "I think I could use some time alone."

She looked at him a long moment, chest tender, heart bruised. "Are you going to be angry with me all night?" she whispered.

"I'm not going to be happy with you, no."

"But you're going to be like this?"

Finally she had his attention, and the look he gave her cut to the core. "As long as you are like this, yes."

Her hands shook as she adjusted her grip on her skirt. "I just wanted to be with you, Thomas. And I'm sorry—"

"But you're not sorry. You're only sorry that I haven't given you a warmer reception. But I didn't want you here. I didn't want you to make this trip, and not because you can't ride, but it's not appropriate, Ellie. I'm here to work, not play house. I don't like being distracted, and I don't appreciate being disrespected."

She exhaled hard, feeling as if he'd punched her.

So that was it. That was why he was angry.

He wasn't worried about her. He didn't care that she'd made an effort to be with him, and to prove she could handle the rigors of the trip. He just didn't want her here. It wasn't *appropriate*.

"YOU DIDN'T MARRY a city girl," she said roughly, her voice trembling with anger and hurt. "I was not raised to be cooped up in a house. I was raised outside, riding, shooting my gun, being adventurous, and free. And I'll learn to cook for you, Thomas. I'll even try to be a good housekeeper to please you. But I'm not ever going to stop being me. And if that bothers you, or embarrasses you, then that's your problem, not mine, as I've no interest in being your convenient wife!"

"A convenient wife? Is that what you call yourself?" He laughed as he ran a hand through his crisp black hair. "Oh, sweetheart, forgive me, but you, love, have been anything but convenient. You approached me. You practically begged me to marry you. You turned my world upside down. I was happy before. I was content before. I had peace before. So don't talk to me about being convenient, because in my eyes, you are nothing but inconvenient."

Her heart pounded in her chest. She was more devastated than he'd ever know. "I appreciate your honesty," she said when she could find her voice. "I'll be honest, too. I think it's unfair and wildly inappropriate that you're so determined to squash the Burnett in me. That's the best part of me, Thomas. That's the part of me you should admire most." And then she walked away, eager to hand the berries over to Mrs. Harrison and then even more eager to get her horse and head back home.

THOMAS WALKED ALONG the stream, jumping from rock to rock, trying to burn off his frustration, not wanting to return to the campsite until he was in a better mood.

He knew he'd hurt Ellie's feelings, but he was worn out, tired from tension and drama. He didn't want to punish her, he didn't want to be cruel, but he wasn't comfortable giving her the same freedom and independence she experienced living with her father.

She wouldn't understand, but he felt more responsible for her well-being than her father had, because Thomas was the outsider. Thomas didn't have the benefit of being a family member. If something happened to her, people would judge him. People would blame him. And he would also blame himself.

As it was, he worried about her, every second of every day. He was anxious leaving her each morning, and he remained troubled until he returned to her each night. He worried about someone stopping by the house during the day, and Ellie setting off on her own, and then having trouble. He knew she carried a gun, and he was sure she could use it, but there were dangers where a gun was of no use.

Floods, storms, fires, illnesses.

Snow.

Ice.

Lightning.

Thomas ran a hand across his face, feeling half-mad.

How had he thought this marriage would work? How had he imagined he could protect Ellie when he couldn't protect his own family?

How could he save Ellie if he couldn't save Eliza, and Eliza wasn't nearly as headstrong or rebellious as Ellie?

SHE'D LEFT THE house for the mountain before seven, and it

had taken her until midafternoon to reach the camp site. It would take at least seven hours to get back home. Ellie glanced at the sky as Oisin's hooves sent a shower of pebbles down the slope. With luck, she'd be off the mountain by dark, and then it'd just be another hour to the house, and she wasn't worried about crossing the pasture by moonlight. She knew the property and knew where to ride. Oisin knew his way home, too, and he'd get her there safely.

It wasn't the trip that worried her, and she didn't waste more than a moment's thought on wolves, or bears, or being accosted by a stranger because she had her shotgun and her pistol and both were loaded and handy should she need them. She'd use them, too, if the situation required, as her father had drummed into her the necessity to be smart and survive.

Her father had taught her many invaluable skills but he'd never told her anything useful about love or men, or marriage, and right now she needed advice and a sympathetic ear, someone who could give her pointers on how to manage a proud, stubborn man like Thomas Sheenan.

It wouldn't be appropriate to ask Mrs. Baxter, and Johnna was in town and still unmarried. Ellie chewed the inside of her cheek, wondering if it would be too inappropriate to seek out Johanna's sister-in-law, McKenna Frasier, Sinclair's wife.

Ellie and McKenna were not friends, but Ellie was desperate and her heart felt close to breaking. She needed to understand what she was doing wrong, and McKenna was a strong woman, and an independent one. If anyone might have some suggestions for dealing with an alpha male, it'd be her.

THOMAS HAD BEEN livid when he walked back into camp an hour later, and discovered that Ellie and Oisin were gone.

It had taken him several long seconds to process that she'd handed over the berries and left.

His hands balled into fists as Harrison apologized, saying they'd all thought Thomas knew, and that he'd given Ellie permission to return.

At another time, Thomas might have laughed at the idea of him giving Ellie permission to do anything. But as it was now, there was nothing laughable about the situation. It would be dark hours before Ellie returned home and he was all too well aware of the dangers of the rugged terrain.

Thomas saddled Crockett and was off as soon as possible.

In the distance, he could hear the howl of a coyote, and then the answering howl of another coyote.

Thank God they were coyotes and not wolves.

But a pack of coyotes wouldn't fear attacking a lone female. Thomas prayed she was on her horse, and alert. He prayed she wouldn't have any trouble on her return, and every mile he rode without a sign of her or Oisin seemed to be a good omen. But he wouldn't be able to relax until he saw her at home, safe.

And then, he would give her hell.

What has she been thinking?

Or more to the point, did she ever think? She was one of the brightest, most accomplished women he had ever met. But, good God, she lacked even a sliver of common sense.

Deciding to trail after him had been a terrible decision on her part. Not just because he had told her no, but because she'd traveled all that way—eight hours at least—all on her own, putting her into all kinds of danger. And then when he was upset, instead of waiting the storm out, she turned around and went right back down the steep mountain, again by herself.

Did she not understand he was worried about her? Did she not understand that her safety was the most important thing to him?

He wouldn't be able to live with himself if something happened to her. She was his. His to cherish, and his to protect.

And then he refused to think anymore, shutting down all thought, smashing all fear, determined to focus only on his goal, and his destination.

He just needed to get home. He just needed to see that Ellie was safe and where she was supposed to be.

IT WAS MIDNIGHT when Thomas finally reached the ranch.

The house was dark. The barn was dark as well, which was how it should be. He felt a rush of relief, thinking everything looked snug and quiet. He tethered Crockett to the back porch, before heading into the house.

He climbed the stairs quickly, battling his temper, not wanting another heated exchange with her at this late hour. They'd have a serious talk in the morning, but for now, he just wanted to ease the panic that had been thudding through his veins for the past seven and a half hours.

The door to her bedroom was open. The bed was empty, the pink quilt smooth, the pillows plump.

She wasn't home. She wasn't here.

He inhaled sharply at the jagged lance of pain, feeling as if a switchblade had just been jammed between his ribs.

For a split-second, he felt violently ill, his worry so intense that he nearly punched the wall, and then he was running down the stairs, and across the yard, throwing open the barn to check the stalls. No sign of her horse. The saddle wasn't on the wall.

She'd never even made it home.

The world narrowed, and all thought ceased. He couldn't see, either, blinded by rage—*he'd told her not to go, he'd told her it was too dangerous*—and then fear—*he couldn't lose her*—and then finally grim determination. *There was no way in hell he would lose her.*

He went to the bunkhouse and pounded on the door, shouting at the young cowhands to wake. When the door opened, he told them to dress and saddle up as they were going to look for Mrs. Sheenan, who'd never made it back from Emigrant Peak.

One of the young hands squinted out at the dark. "Shouldn't we at least wait till daybreak? I don't know how we'd ever find her without any light."

"Do you want a job here?" Thomas ground out. "If you do, saddle up, and if you don't, get the hell off my ranch."

Then, minutes later, both hands were on their horses, joining Thomas as they cantered away from the house and barn, heading east toward the mountain's dark hulking shape. "We'll spread out once we reach the base of the mountain," Thomas told them. "I don't know if she's hurt, or just lost, or if Oisin went lame. Keep your ears and eyes open and hopefully the next time I see you my wife will have been found."

AT DAWN, McKENNA made Ellie a cup of hot, sweet tea while Sinclair saddled Oisin and then McKenna gave her a hug and Ellie was on her way home, with Sinclair as an escort.

Ellie hadn't wanted an escort, but Sinclair wouldn't hear of her leaving and riding home without someone to see her safely back.

"I've traveled between the two houses plenty of times in the past," Ellie answered. "I don't know why you're making a fuss now."

"If the roles were reversed and it was McKenna heading home, I would hope your husband would see her safely back."

"That's because McKenna can't ride or shoot half as well as me."

His lips twisted as he checked his smile. "No, it's because I love McKenna and I'd never forgive myself if something happened to her."

Ellie didn't answer and Sinclair said nothing else until the old Burnett Ranch house came into view. "McKenna didn't tell me everything that you two discussed last night, and I don't want to know, but clearly you came over in need of some female company and I hoped she could help."

"She was very kind, and she gave me some good advice."

"I'm glad." He hesitated. "You're strong, and that's good, but you have to remember that men have pride."

"I know. Archibald Burnett was my father."

"He was a great man, too."

"He was," she agreed.

"And you put him on a pedestal."

She shot him a side glance but said nothing.

"It's awfully hard, if not impossible, for any man to fill shoes that big," he added quietly, "but I admire Sheenan for trying."

ELLIE COULDN'T GET Sinclair's words out of her head as she climbed the staircase to her room. She'd never quite thought of the situation that way, but he was right. She'd adored her father and he'd been her hero, and it couldn't have been easy for Thomas to take on the ranch responsibilities, and her, particularly on the heels of her father's death.

Reeling with exhaustion, she tugged off her riding boots and struggled out of her dress. She threw herself down on her bed in her petticoats, so very glad Sinclair had insisted on unsaddling Oisin and rubbing him down before making sure he had food and water before he left. She would have done it herself if Sinclair hadn't offered, but she was so saddle sore right now and ached in every muscle and joint.

It was too much riding for one day.

It was too much heartache for one day.

All she wanted to do was collapse into bed and sleep forever.

She pulled one of the crisp cool pillows beneath her cheek and closed her eyes, thinking only of sleep—

"Where the hell have you been?"

Thomas's deep, rough voice jolted her awake. Ellie lunged into a sitting position, her hands flying up as if to protect herself. "What?"

"Where have you been all night?"

She gave her head a groggy shake. "I've been here."

"You were not here. I followed you off the mountain last night and you didn't come home and then I see Douglas riding away from the house—"

"He escorted me home, that's all."

"And why did he need to escort you home? Were you lost on his property?"

"No. I rode over to the Douglas's to speak to McKenna."

"And why would you do that? You don't even like her."

"I don't dislike her."

"She stole your fiancé. You're not friends. You've never been friends."

"She also came to our wedding, as she's my best friend's sister-in-law."

"You didn't go to see McKenna Douglas. You went to see her husband."

Ellie stiffened, outraged. It was one thing for him to be in a foul temper, but another to accuse her of something frankly adulterous. "I did not! I didn't even speak to him last night. We only spoke when he escorted me home."

"Was he up here? Was he in this room?"

"No! *No.* Absolutely not."

"I knew you still loved him."

For a minute she just stared at him, baffled by the accusations. Where was this coming from? How could he even think such a thing? "What is wrong with you? Have you lost your mind? There is nothing between Sinclair and me—"

"It doesn't look that way, Ellie. It looks as if you want what you can't have. But then you always want what you can't have."

She applauded. "Yes! So true. You couldn't be more right."

His brow lowered and his arms crossed over his chest. "I'm not in the mood for games."

"Well, neither am I. Because I do want what I can't have, and what I want is you, Thomas Sheenan, you awful, ridiculous, hardheaded Irishman! I want *you*. Because I love *you*. But you don't believe in feelings and emotion and whenever I get even a little bit close to you you push me away—" She broke off and gulped a great breath as she grabbed her pillow and threw it at him, and then grabbed the other pillow and threw that one, too.

"And for you to even suggest that I have any interest in Sinclair when all I want is *you*, and to be with *you*, after I spent seven and a half miserable hours riding up that damn mountain to find you, only to have you say those cruel, hurtful things—"

She broke off again, tears filling her eyes. "Shame on you, Thomas Sheenan! Shame on you because I have only loved two men in my life. My father. And *you*."

THOMAS STOOD ROOTED to the spot, jaw clenched, teeth aching. His stomach hurt, as though he'd swallowed a jar full of nails. "You don't know what you're saying," he said lowly, stiffly, forcing himself to speak.

"Oh, I do, I know exactly what I'm saying, and exactly

what you're not saying." She drew a hysterical breath. "You don't love me and you'll never love me and I'm the fool because I fell for you even before you married me. I fell for you that night in December when I saw you on the firetruck and in that crazy, horrifying moment where everything went wrong, something also went right. I lost Sinclair, and found *you*."

She reached up to dash away the tears but she couldn't catch them and they spilled, one after the other. "I wish I didn't love you. It'd be so much easier if I didn't care—"

And then Thomas, who wasn't good with words, and didn't trust words, did the only thing that made sense.

He went to the bed and picked her up even as she swung wildly at him, punching him in the chest, and flipped her on her back, pinning her thrashing legs, and grabbing hold of her fists and he kissed her.

He kissed her not only to silence her painful stream of words, but to calm her and stop the tears.

The kiss was hot and fierce, part punishment and part desperation. Thomas had been out of his mind with worry. All night he'd battled his fear and how it ate at his heart, torturing him with outcomes that he couldn't accept. Nothing could happen to her. Nothing.

She had to be okay, she had to be fine. It was the only way, it was the only acceptable outcome. Thomas had lost people before. But he wasn't going to lose Ellie. He wouldn't even contemplate such a thing. Ellie was his... his world, his heart, his future.

"You can't do that to me again," he said, against her mouth, his hands cradling her face. He could feel the tears sliding down her temples into her hair. "You can't just disappear like that."

"I was going home. You didn't want me."

"I always want you," he answered, kissing her again, deeply, his tongue finding the soft recesses of her mouth, and hearing her whimper as he stroked the delicate skin with all the nerve endings.

He loved her low whimper and the way she arched against him as he slid his hand down her hips and then between her thighs.

"You can't have me, though," she answered huskily. "You can't just take me when you want me."

"But I want you all the time." He lifted his head and gazed down into her luscious green eyes. He'd prayed he'd find her in one piece, but he'd prayed before for a miracle and it hadn't been granted. "I was so worried, Ellie. You have no idea."

It was true. He'd been heartsick, so heartsick he'd felt poisoned all the way through.

And then when he saw Douglas riding away from the house, Thomas had wanted to destroy his neighbor. He'd wanted to beat him to a pulp but Sinclair was too far away and Thomas was too intent on finding Ellie.

"You are mine," he murmured, still studying her beautiful face, as if trying to memorize it forever. He traced the winged eyebrows and the small straight nose and then her full, generous mouth. "My bride. My wife. My family. You're all I have, and all I want."

Her lower lip quivered. "But you hate feelings, and you don't want to love me."

"I'm afraid it's too late for that. You weaseled your way into my heart a long, long time ago."

"*Weaseled?*"

He smiled at her indignant tone and lowered his head, slowly kissing her, a kiss so hot and hungry she wound her arms around his neck and pulled him down, even closer.

"Is charmed better?" he teased, one hand skimming over her hipbone, and then finding warm soft skin beneath the petticoat.

"Yes, but we both know I'm not charming, at least, I wasn't charming toward you."

"And why is that?"

"Because I liked you too much, and you didn't like me."

"Oh, I liked you, quite a bit." His fingers slipped between her thighs and found her where she was warm and damp. He stroked her until she was breathless and arching up against him. "But I was out of your league, sweetheart. What could I offer you? Nothing."

Her nails bit into his shoulders and she closed her eyes, panting as the pleasure built. He watched her lovely face as she struggled to retain control.

"I should have said no to your proposal, Ellie. I knew I didn't deserve you, but God help me, I wanted you. And I will want you forever." And then his mouth covered hers, drinking in her cry as she climaxed.

ELLIE SLOWLY OPENED her eyes, and frowned at the bright sunlight pouring through her open bedroom window. Taking a breath, she felt the weight of Thomas's arm around her, holding her firmly to him, his knee between her thighs.

Something had happened… what had happened?

And then it all started coming back to her.

The trip up the mountain, the tearful ride back, the conversation with McKenna and then Thomas returning, and accusing her of having Sinclair in her room…

She remembered how she told him everything, and how she'd practically shouted that she loved him.

Ellie cringed, remembering that part. She wished she hadn't said quite everything, and she really wish she hadn't shouted all that about loving him. It was so embarrassing and awkward since emotion wasn't his thing. Now all she wanted to do was escape but Thomas's arm was ridiculously heavy and, despite giving it a shove, she couldn't get it to move.

"Going somewhere?" he asked, his voice deep but not at all sleepy.

She glanced over her shoulder at him. His dark gaze met hers and he lifted a brow.

"I'm going downstairs. I'm sure you must be hungry or something."

"And you are such an excellent cook."

She would have punched him if she had a free hand.

"So violent," he teased, rolling her onto her back as if she weighed nothing. He straddled her hips, his hands catching her wrists and holding them down.

"Because you make me angry!"

"What did I do now?"

"How could you accuse me of behaving improperly with Sinclair? How could you think so little of me to even suggest such a thing?"

Thomas's smile faded. He released her hands but didn't move off her. "That was wrong of me. I shouldn't have said that. I'm sorry."

"But why did you?"

His broad shoulders shifted. "Because I know you'd wanted to marry Douglas. He was your first choice—"

"Only because I hadn't met you yet." Her eyes burned and she struggled to keep herself from falling apart again. "You are my first choice."

He made a rough sound. "You don't need to say that. I'm not that fragile."

"But it's true. You are the only man I've ever proposed to."

"Because you'd run out of time."

"Because I'd finally found the right one."

"I brought nothing into this marriage, Ellie girl."

She swallowed against the lump filling her throat. *Ellie girl.* It was the same thing her father used to call her. "You brought exactly what I needed," she whispered, blinking to clear her vision. "You brought *you.*"

He said nothing, his dark gaze shuttered, his expression impossible to read.

"Thomas," she whispered, trying to smile, wanting so very much to reach him, and reassure him. "You are what I need. And even if you don't love me—"

"Stop."

"It's okay, because I'd rather have you and have something of you, than nothing—"

He stretched over her, his mouth covering hers, stealing her words and her air and her pain.

He kissed her until her heart slowed and her veins felt full of sunshine and honey.

"I love you," he said roughly, lifting his head to look her in the eyes. "It's that simple, and that complicated."

"Why complicated?"

"Because I wouldn't survive losing you. I'm not going to do this life without you."

She smiled through her tears. "You don't have to. I'm here. We're here. Together."

"Life is harsh."

"But also beautiful."

"I don't trust God."

"Oh, I do. He brought me you." Her tears were falling again and she struggled against the overwhelming emotion. She reached up to stroke his hard, handsome face. "And how I love you. You have no idea."

He turned his lips into her hand, kissing her palm. "You say everything I'd like to say. I wish I had more words, I struggle to find the right words."

"Can I help you with the words as its obvious I have plenty of them?"

He smiled crookedly. "Please do."

"I'll ask the question, and you answer. How is that?"

"Fine."

"I'm not actually going to ask a lot. I just need to know one thing. Do you love me?"

His dark eyes met hers and held. "With all my heart."

Her own heart thumped hard in response. She exhaled. "That's all I need to know."

"Are you sure?" He rolled over, bringing her with him so that she was now on top of him. "No more questions? No worries or concerns? Is everything truly, finally clear?"

"Well, maybe just another question."

"Okay."

"When did you know you first loved me?"

"Last December when I saw you rushing after Douglas, begging him not to leave you."

Her jaw dropped, eyes widening.

He nodded. "You were the most beautiful woman I'd

ever seen, and I thought, if you were mine, I'd never let you go. And so when you proposed, I couldn't refuse you, even though I knew I didn't deserve you. I had the chance to make you mine, and I did."

Warmth rushed through her, warmth and hope and happiness so bright that she couldn't quite take it all in. "Thank goodness Sinclair didn't want me."

"I know why he didn't."

She arched a brow.

He cupped the back of her head and pulled her down to him, murmuring, "Because you were made for me."

She looked into his eyes and nodded, and then nodded again. "I love you, Thomas Sheenan."

"I love you, Ellie Burnett."

"Sheenan," she corrected huskily. "Ellie Burnett Sheenan. And I wouldn't have it any other way."

EPILOGUE

ELLIE AND THOMAS Sheenan were a truly happy couple. They loved deeply, and fought infrequently, with fights usually resolved by Thomas carrying Ellie off to the new master bedroom he'd built for her downstairs, the room filled with windows, and a huge four-poster bed and a handsome river rock fireplace to keep his Ellie girl warm on even the coldest of Montana mornings.

He loved her in bed, and out of bed, and it wasn't long before they had their first child, and then four more.

Four of their five babies grew into adulthood, and those four—William, James, Elizabeth, and Archie—married and had children, giving Ellie and Thomas seventeen grandchildren, including an Archibald, Jr and a little Biddy.

Ellie never did love cooking, but she mastered two dishes for her husband, Irish soda bread and his favorite steak & stout pie.

She never could resist him and he adored the ground she walked on.

They celebrated their fiftieth wedding anniversary on April 5, 1940 with all their children and grandchildren joining them for dinner and cake and champagne at the original Burnett-Sheenan homestead.

Thomas had always said he couldn't live without her, and thankfully he never had to.

THE END

The Paradise Valley Ranch Series

Book 1: *Away in Montana*
McKenna Douglas' story

Book 2: *Married in Montana*
Ellie Sheenan's story

Book 3: *Home in Montana*
Coming soon

New York Times bestselling author Jane Porter's contemporary romance series....

The Taming of the Sheenans

The Sheenans are six powerful wealthy brothers from Marietta, Montana. They are big, tough, rugged men, and as different as the Montana landscape.

Christmas at Copper Mountain
Book 1: Brock Sheenan's story

Tycoon's Kiss
Book 2: Troy Sheenan's story

The Kidnapped Christmas Bride
Book 3: Trey Sheenan's story

Taming of the Bachelor
Book 4: Dillion Sheenan's story

A Christmas Miracle for Daisy
Book 5: Cormac Sheenan's story

The Lost Sheenan's Bride
Book 6: Shane Sheenan's story

Available now at your favorite online retailer!

About the Author

New York Times and USA Today bestselling author of forty-nine romances and women's fiction titles, **Jane Porter** has been a finalist for the prestigious RITA award five times and won in 2014 for Best Novella with her story, Take Me, Cowboy, from Tule Publishing. Today, Jane has over 12 million copies in print, including her wildly successful, Flirting With Forty, picked by Redbook as its Red Hot Summer Read, and reprinted six times in seven weeks before being made into a Lifetime movie starring Heather Locklear. A mother of three sons, Jane holds an MA in Writing from the University of San Francisco and makes her home in sunny San Clemente, CA with her surfer husband and two dogs.

Thank you for reading

Married in Montana

If you enjoyed this book, you can find more from all our great authors at TulePublishing.com, or from your favorite online retailer.

TULE
PUBLISHING

34366754R00168

Made in the USA
Lexington, KY
22 March 2019